the Cheetah girls

Dorinda Gets a Groove

Deborah Gregory

JUMP AT THE SUN

HYPERION PAPERBACKS FOR CHILDREN

NEW YORK

Fashion credits: Photography by Charlie Pizzarello.
Models: Davida Williams, Laura Luther, Sabrina Millen,
Sonya Millen, Imani Parks, and Brandi Stewart. Apparel
by: Betsey Johnson, Daang Goodman for Tripp, NYC, P.
Fields, Nicole Miller. Hair by Julie McIntosh. Makeup
by Kathleen Herch and Tasha Vila. Fashion styling by
Nole Martin.

Printed in the United States of America
First Edition
 3 5 7 9 10 8 6 4 2
This book is set in 12-point Palatino.
ISBN 0-7868-1477-2
Library of Congress Catalog Card Number: 00-108994
Visit www.cheetahgirls.com

For my Hollywood peeps, Walter Franks,
who puts duckets in the banks
while always giving thanks
to the creator and initiator
of his theatrical flow,
which makes imitators take notice
of his comedy show
and act like they know
that this is one hot dog
who ain't full of beans and schemes
in the land of dreams!

The Cheetah Girls Credo

To earn my spots and rightful place in the world, I solemnly swear to honor and uphold the Cheetah Girls oath:

- Cheetah Girls don't litter, they glitter. I will help my family, friends, and other Cheetah Girls whenever they need my love, support, or a *really* big hug.

- All Cheetah Girls are created equal, but we are not alike. We come in different sizes, shapes, and colors, and hail from different cultures. I will not judge others by the color of their spots, but by their character.

- A true Cheetah Girl doesn't spend more time doing her hair than her homework. Hair extensions may be career extensions, but talent and skills will pay my bills.

- True Cheetah Girls *can* achieve without a weave—or a wiggle, jiggle, or a giggle. I promise to rely (mostly) on my brains, heart, and courage to reach my cheetah-licious potential!

- A brave Cheetah Girl isn't afraid to admit when she's scared. I promise to get on my knees and summon the growl power of the Cheetah Girls who came before me—including my mom, grandmoms, and the Supremes—and ask them to help me be strong.

- All Cheetah Girls make mistakes. I promise to admit when I'm wrong and will work to make it right. I'll also say I'm sorry, even when I don't want to.

- Grown-ups are not always right, but they are bigger, older, and louder. I will treat my teachers, parents, and people of authority with respect—and expect them to do the same!

🐾 True Cheetah Girls don't run with wolves or hang with hyenas. True Cheetahs pick much better friends. I will not try to get other people's approval by acting like a copycat.

🐾 To become the Cheetah Girl that only *I* can be, I promise not to follow anyone else's dreams but my own. No matter how much I quiver, shake, shiver, and quake!

🐾 Cheetah Girls were born for adventure. I promise to learn a language other than my own and travel around the world to meet my fellow Cheetah Girls.

the Cheetah Girls

Chapter 1

Today is the first day Chanel is out of her house since her ballerina audition, when she broke her tailbone and sprained her ankle. I can tell she is so excited she could do a pirouette right here on Thirty-ninth Street. I don't know how Chanel managed to stay home for a week—getting ice packs on her butt and resting with her ankle elevated on a pillow—because she can be really restless. I mean, Chanel probably has more energy than all the dancers in the American Ballet Theatre put together! Of course, now that she's really messed up her ankle, the doctor says the only pirouettes she'll be doing are in her daydreams.

Well, Chanel's not the only one glad to be out of the house. When I left for school this morning, I heard my foster mother, Mrs. Bosco, talking on the phone with someone down at the foster care agency. So I know something is about to go down, and I'm in no hurry to go home and find out what it is. See, with ten foster brothers and sisters, there is *always* some new drama unfolding at my house.

Right now, though, we're waiting outside this fancy-schmancy restaurant for Ms. Dorothea, who is Galleria's mom, Chanel's godmother, *and* the Cheetah Girls' manager. I guess you could say we are triple lucky. The Cheetah Girls, of course, is the name of our singing group—but we are as tight as a crew can be: besides little ole me—Dorinda "Do' Re Mi" Rogers—there's our ringleader, Galleria "Bubbles" Garibaldi; Chanel "Chuchie" Simmons (also known as Miss Cuchifrita Ballerina); and the "boostin' Houston twins," Aquanette and Anginette Walker.

We're getting together tonight because Ms. Dorothea is treating us to dinner. She knows how hard it's been for Chanel to stay off her feet—and for us, too, because we can't rehearse until Chanel gets better.

Looking up at the awning, I try to pronounce the restaurant's name but keep bumbling the last word. *"Le Kosher Cha-too?"*

"No, Do', it's Cha*teau*—as in 'act like you *know*,'" Galleria says, with emphasis, so I'll get the drift. "Mom must be pulling a Rapunzel, and weaving the fabrics herself on a loom," she hisses in between loud pops of bubble gum— the habit that earned Bubbles her nickname to the max.

Ms. Dorothea left early this morning to shop for fabrics for her spring collection. See, Ms. Dorothea has this dope boutique, called Toto in New York . . . Fun in Diva Sizes, down in SoHo near where Chanel lives. Ms. Dorothea is definitely my inspiration, because I love designing clothes—as much as I love dancing and being in the Cheetah Girls.

"Miss Cuchifrita Ballerina, are you getting tired?" Galleria asks, concerned. We gave Chanel her second nickname *before* her pirouette caper backfired and landed her in the emergency room. See, when we got back from Houston, Chanel decided to give her ballerina moves a test run by auditioning for the Junior Corps Division of American Ballet Theatre. She got so nervous at the audition, though, that she went leaping across the floor and landed right on her back!

I think Chanel is relieved that she has to hang up her pointe shoes for good, because now she has to face the fact that she's stuck with *us*. I mean, we're *all* kinda scared about being in a singing group. It's not an easy-breezy ride on Hit Records Street, you know—it's a lot harder than we thought it was gonna be.

"Coming through, ladies, coming through!" yells this big, gruffy guy, startling me out of my thoughts. I turn to see Mr. Gruffy and two other tough-looking men, all wearing the same blue jumpsuit uniform and wheeling a huge cart filled with big rolls of fabric right in our direction.

Aqua is so busy gabbing to her sister, Angie, that she isn't paying attention. I push her aside gently, so she won't get knocked off the sidewalk and end up with "street gravy" splattered all over her nice powder-blue skirt and white blouse.

The men roll past us like they're maneuvering a Mack truck in a war zone. I turn to the twins and chuckle, "Now you *know* we're back in New York."

"You're sure enough right, Miss Dorinda," Aqua says, rolling her eyes in the direction of the "three gruffateers."

I look up at all the gloomy gray buildings with dusty windows and wonder what the people inside are doing—cutting patterns, sewing on sleeves, fitting clothes on mannequin figures. See, this is the heart of the Garment District, and buyers from all over the world come here to see what the Big Apple has to offer in the fashion department. Yup, the Big Apple has got it like that.

When I look down, I see a big cheetah hat sticking up from the crowd of people rushing to get home from work. "There she is!" I say to Galleria, pointing down the block. "I can spot your mom's spots anywhere."

When she gets close, I can see that Ms. Dorothea's face is shiny with perspiration. "Sorry I'm late, darlings, but I've just been haggling for dear life with these sales reps. You wouldn't believe what they were trying to charge for wool—*blend*." Ms. Dorothea takes a deep breath.

"Hi, *Madrina*!" Chanel says excitedly. She bends over to kiss her godmother, while trying to balance her pink plastic pocketbook and pair of crutches at the same time. Chanel loves purses, but I love the cheetah backpacks Ms. Dorothea gave all of us when we became the Cheetah Girls. That's what I always carry when I'm rolling.

"Hi, *Madrina*," yells Pucci, Chanel's younger brother, who has also come along for the supa-dupa dinner.

"Hello, Pucci. After you, Monsieur and Mademoiselle," says Ms. Dorothea. She opens the door of the restaurant, and makes a grand gesture with her arm for Pucci and Chanel to enter first—like they're Prince Charming and Cinderella walking down the red carpet to the Ball. I guess it is kinda special, since this is the first time the Cheetah Girls have all been out together since we got back from Houston.

"This is really nice!" Pucci exclaims when we walk inside. Ms. Dorothea picked this restaurant, and she has diva-size taste, if you know what I'm saying.

"Juanita, I think you're going to owe me one after this," Ms. Dorothea says to Chanel's mom,

Mrs. Simmons, who has also been invited for dinner. I can tell Ms. Dorothea is really proud of her restaurant selection.

Pucci looks so cute, strutting ahead of me in his three-piece burgundy corduroy suit. "Pucci, you look really nice," I exclaim, gently touching his shoulder.

"This is the suit *Madrina* gave me for my birthday," Pucci says proudly, sticking out his chest like a peacock.

"I love pinwale," I say, rubbing his shoulder and looking admiringly at Ms. Dorothea. We both could spend hours looking at fabrics and touching them.

"But I'm not a pin-whale!" Pucci blurts back at me, grinning, then looks at Galleria for approval. I can tell Pucci really likes Galleria, and really looks up to her in the snaps department.

"I know, Pucci," I say, humoring him. "I was talking about the fabric—pinwale means small-ribbed corduroy."

"*I* know that," Pucci shoots back, raising his left eyebrow and cocking his head.

"You did not," Galleria says, rubbing his bald head. Pucci's head really does look like a pool ball, now that he's had it shaved clean again.

As the hostess shows us to our table, I can't help but notice that we look, well, different from the other people in the restaurant—and that's not because of Chanel's crutches, if you know what I'm saying. Ms. Dorothea doesn't seem to notice, because she waltzes by the tables with her head held so high it almost touches the ceiling. She's like the head cheetah in an empty desert—there's no way she could hide her spots! I wish I was tall like her—then everybody would respect me, too. I guess I'm still a cub, because I put my head down as we walk by this big round table, with ladies wearing pearl necklaces and matching earrings. Then I shove my hands in my jacket, and fidget with my fingers inside the deep pockets.

The hostess seats us at a big round table, too, with a nice white linen tablecloth—not paper or plastic, okay? I get nervous again, because I don't want to spill anything on it. Even the napkins are linen. I wonder how they keep everything so clean. Daintily unfolding the linen napkin, I place it carefully over my lap. Chanel taught me that little "magic trick." Well, it was a magic trick to me, because I didn't have any table manners until the rest of the Cheetah

Girls taught me how to "slice on the nice tip"!

I glance at the table next to us and notice that the boys are wearing some sort of beanies on their heads. I wonder what those are? Then I look around and notice that almost *all* the boys in the restaurant are wearing the *same* thing on their heads, pinned in place with bobby pins.

Angie and Aqua whisper something to each other, which is probably why Ms. Dorothea pipes up. "I wanted to treat you girls to something different. This is what you call a kosher French restaurant."

We all look at each other, and I can tell that none of us knows what she's talking about. At least Pucci has the nerve to speak up. "How come all the boys are wearing those things on their heads?"

Ms. Dorothea chuckles at Pucci, so I relax into my chair. "Those are yarmulkes, Pucci. It's a sign of reverence for males of the Jewish faith to wear them in public."

"Oh," Pucci replies, then shrugs his shoulders. "How come the girls don't wear them, too?"

"That's a good question, and one I don't know the answer to," Ms. Dorothea explains, smiling at the lady next to us with all the kids.

Now that Pucci has broken the ice, I decide to ask a question too. "So, um, what does kosher mean?"

"Well, it means that the restaurant serves food according to Jewish dietary laws, such as, they don't serve meat and dairy products in the same meal, or sometimes not even in the same restaurant, and the meat is only from birds, or animals that have split hooves and chew their cud, like cows—but definitely not pigs."

We all look at Ms. Dorothea like she's suddenly become a farmer.

"You mean like giraffes, too?" Pucci asks giggling.

"Exactly, Pucci—except I don't think you'll find any giraffe dishes on the menu. But you will find duck, steak, bison."

I wonder what a bison is, but I'm certainly not going to ask. I'll look it up tomorrow in school. As if reading my mind, though, Ms. Dorothea adds quickly, "Bison, of course, is buffalo meat."

"Buffalo meat?" Pucci says, squinching up his nose. "Yuck."

Mrs. Simmons throws Pucci a look.

"Nonetheless, you will find the food quite

fabulous here," Ms. Dorothea says, looking over her menu at Mrs. Simmons.

Taking her cue, we each pick up our menus and gaze upon the goodies. *Everything on the menu is in French!* I realize, staring at the type and panicking, until I look closer and notice that the English version is in tiny letters below each selection. Whew! I sure wasn't gonna try to pronounce anything to the waiter in French, if you know what I'm saying.

"So, Chanel, how are you feeling?" Ms. Dorothea asks her goddaughter.

"Fine! I'm so happy to be out of the house!" Chanel says cheerfully.

"I caught her trying to do leg lifts in the exercise studio this morning," Mrs. Simmons announces to all of us.

"Keep it up and you won't be able to perform in the Def Duck showcase that I'm setting up—again," Ms. Dorothea warns her. See, when Chanel sprained her ankle, we had to postpone doing a showcase for the East Coast executives at Def Duck Records. Ms. Dorothea was gonna hook us up with a showcase at the Leaping Frog Lounge downtown.

"So, Dorinda—how's your sister, Tiffany?"

Ms. Dorothea suddenly asks me. Now why did she have to bring that up? See, not too long ago, I didn't even know I had a half sister named Tiffany. She and I have the same birth mother, but Tiffany was adopted as a baby, and I was sent to foster care. Then, last month, Tiffany came and found me—and now I'm not sure I want to deal with this new drama, you know what I'm saying?

"Oh, she's okay," I say quickly, then change the subject back again and fidget with the menu. "When are we going to do that Cheetah Girls showcase, Ms. Dorothea?"

"As soon as Chanel's able to walk on stage without a crutch. Don't worry—the A&R people are panting like puppies over the idea." Ms. Dorothea sips from her glass with a satisfied smirk. *She* was the one who thought of approaching Def Duck Records with the idea of putting together a showcase, so the East Coast executives could get a whiff of our flavor. Then maybe they'll be motivated to put us in the studio with big-cheese producer Mouse Almighty—the man who holds the key to our future. See, if such an important producer picks the right tracks for us, then we sound good—

and if we sound good, then the tracks will test well, and Def Duck will give us a record deal— that's what I'm talking about.

"I sure hope Chanel's ankle heals fast," I say, chuckling. Then I get embarrassed, because I don't want her to think I'm being insensitive about her situation. Chanel and I are really tight, you know what I'm saying? I smile at her, and she smiles back, so I guess everything's cool.

"Don't you worry, Do' Re Mi, I'm gonna be back in Cheetah Girl form in no time," Chanel says, then looks cautiously at her mother. "You'll see, *Mami*."

Uh-oh. I hope we're not going to spin *that* record again. See, Chanel's mom is looking for any reason to yank her out of the Cheetah Girls because she doesn't approve of this whole girl-group thing. She thinks we'll ruin our futures or something.

Luckily, something catches Mrs. Simmons's attention. I turn to see what she's looking at— it's the waiter, who has returned and is ready to take our orders.

Afterward, the conversation turns back to the Cheetah Girls—only this time, it's Ms.

Dorothea who's bringing in the noise. "Have you girls heard any more ruckus from that group in Houston?" she asks innocently as we chomp on our food.

"What group?" Mrs. Simmons asks, concerned. *Uh-oh.* Judging from the way Chanel is squirming in her chair, I guess she didn't tell her mother about what happened. Why would she?

We all look at each other, and finally Galleria realizes that someone is gonna have to fill Mrs. Simmons in on the showdown that took place at the Okie-Dokie Corral. "See, Auntie Juanita, we performed with this group called Cash Money Girls, in the Miss Sassy-sparilla contest, and they said that we stole the words from *their* song for *our* song," she explains.

Mrs. Simmons daintily cuts her meat with a knife and fork, and I can tell that she is trying not to say anything. I watch her closely, and cut my steak the same way, but I guess I'm trying too hard, because one of the little red beans flies off the plate and plops onto the pretty white tablecloth! "Sorry," I say, my face turning red. Now I don't know if I'm supposed to pick up the bean or just leave it there.

Chanel beats me to it, sticking her fork into it

and plopping it back on my plate. "It's okay, *mija*," she whispers, then winks at me.

"Copyright infringement. Hmm," Mrs. Simmons finally says.

"Well, I guess you girls learned a new word in your vocabulary—plagiarism." Ms. Dorothea chuckles, then winks.

I know she's right. Galleria and Chanel should have known better than to crib another group's lyrics—'cuz it just looks like we're trying to bite *their* flavor.

All of a sudden, the twins let out a scream in unison: "*AAAAHHH!*" Aqua lifts her feet in the air and looks over in the corner. "We just saw a mouse run by!"

"A mouse?" Mrs. Simmons asks in disbelief.

"*Sí*—a mouse, I saw it too!" Chanel shrieks.

I just sit quiet and be chill. I've seen a lot of mice up in the projects where I live, so I'm not afraid of them at all—but it is kinda strange that a mouse would be hanging out in a nice restaurant like this, you know what I'm saying?

The hostess and the waiter scurry over to our table with a million apologies. "We are terribly sorry. We can't believe that happened. Are you okay?"

"We're fine, darlings," Ms. Dorothea says, trying to take control of the situation.

"Well, please—desserts and after-dinner drinks will be complimentary," the hostess says.

After we accept, Galleria quips, "I wonder if that was Mouse Almighty, trying to find us some tracks for our test demo!"

"I wish it was!" Aqua says, trying not to act scared anymore. "Then at least we could offer *him* a complimentary dessert, too!"

Chapter 2

E ven though it's already dark by the time I hit the courtyard in front of my building, Ms. Keisha is still sitting there with her children, Pookie and Tamela. I can see Ms. Keisha's pink-flowered housecoat peeking out from under her gray plaid overcoat, and her pink bedroom slippers are so fluffy it looks like she's wearing Martian-sized marshmallows on her feet. As I walk up to the bench they're sitting on, I can feel a bad case of the squigglies coming on, because I know she is dying to tell me *something*.

"Betty sure has her hands full now," Ms. Keisha starts in on her story. Betty is the first name of my foster mother, Mrs. Bosco, who doesn't like Ms. Keisha a whole lot. "You didn't come home today after school, did you?" Ms. Keisha asks, but I can tell she already knows the answer.

"No I didn't. 'Member Ms. Dorothea, our manager?"

"Yeah—that lady who was up here dressed like a tiger, at your 'adoption' party—I mean, well you know what I mean," Ms. Keisha says loudly.

"She wears cheetah stuff," I correct her, my cheeks burning from embarrassment. It figures Ms. Keisha found out that my 'adoption' didn't go through.

"Um, she took us out to dinner to this fancy restaurant, and some mouse decided to get in on the action, too," I babble, because I'm scared about what Ms. Keisha is gonna tell me.

"At least he didn't go home hungry—'cuz he sure wouldn't have found anything to eat in my house!" Ms. Keisha snarkles like a hyena. Then Tamela and Pookie let out little hyena snarkles, which is kinda scary, because they sound just like their mother.

"Well, you got a new sister," Ms. Keisha pipes up, finally getting to the point of this joint.

Now I've got a pain in my chest. How does Ms. Keisha know about Tiffany? I can't believe Mrs. Bosco told her! Now Ms. Keisha will tell everybody in the projects that I have an adopted sister! I'll bet Mrs. Bosco invited Tiffany over here behind my back, so she can see how messy and tiny our apartment is!

"You should have seen that child crying—she cried all the way upstairs," Ms. Keisha says, nodding her head.

Why would Tiffany be crying? Why was she *here*? Well, I guess it figures that she would be a big crybaby. She probably gets her way all the time, what with her parents living over on Park Avenue.

"Annie Buckus in 3C says that's the same child that was on the news last week. That's what she said, all right." Ms. Keisha folds her hands in her lap and rocks back and forth. When she sees the alarmed look on my face, she quickly babbles, "I don't know how Annie could remember something like that, but she swears it's the same child. But you know Annie—she never gets anything right."

"Yeah," I say, completely dumbfounded. What could be wrong with Tiffany that she would be on the news?

" 'Member when Gus got robbed across the street, and Annie swore up and down she saw the guy—and that he was a big ole tall guy with an Afro? When the police caught the thief, he looked like a little beady-eyed raccoon—he wasn't nothing like Annie said!"

"No, I don't remember that," I respond, but I'm not really listening to Ms. Keisha. I'm lost in my own thoughts, trying to catch my breath, because it feels like somebody is standing on my chest or something.

"Yeah—that's right, you was too young to 'member that. You're so mature, sometimes I forget you're just a little bitty thing," Ms. Keisha says, chuckling.

I wish Ms. Keisha wouldn't call me little. I *hate* being called little—but now I've gotta find out what's going on, so I ask her nicely, "What was the girl on television for?"

"Annie says that they found the child wandering by herself in Coney Island, over there in Brooklyn. Now you know her mother went and left her there. The child was sitting on the bench wailing for so long, that finally one of the security guards took her to the police station."

Ms. Keisha wraps her coat tighter around her chest. "She got a West Indian accent, too. I could tell, even though she was carrying on and screaming all the way to the elevator."

Now I think Ms. Keisha doesn't know what she's talking about. At least, not Tiffany. "Um, what did the girl look like?" I ask hesitantly.

"Oh, little ole thing with pigtails and a big pout on her face," Ms. Keisha responds.

"Her sneakers were dirty!" Tamela blurts out. "They had holes in them, too."

"Hush up, Tamela—the poor child was probably scared to death, and all you talking about is her sneakers!

Now I *know* she isn't talking about Tiffany. I feel so relieved! "Well, I'd better be going," I say, turning so red I can't even look at Pookie and Tamela.

Ms. Keisha yells after me, "Dorinda, let me know tomorrow if it's the same child Annie saw on the news."

"Oh, right," I say, but now I'm wondering what really is going on upstairs. This must have something to do with what Mrs. Bosco was talking about on the phone this morning.

When I open the apartment door, Twinkie

greets me as usual. Her blond, fuzzy hair is plopping all over the place, and her cheeks are more red than usual. "We got a new sister," she whispers to me, grabbing my arm. "Mr. Bosco is home, too."

I feel the squigglies in my stomach again. I should have known Ms. Keisha was right. She seems to be the only one around here who knows what's going on—because I sure don't!

"That's her," Twinkie says, pointing into the living room at this sad, pouty-faced girl. "She doesn't like us. I don't think she wants to be here."

Neither do I, shrieks a voice inside me, but I give Twinkie a hug and whisper back, "Don't say that, Twinkie. Don't you remember how sad you were when you came here?"

Twinkie nods, and says, "You let me eat all your pretzels."

"That's right," I chuckle. Twinkie's real name is Rita. She has lived with Mrs. Bosco for almost two years, and we have grown very close. I don't know what I would do if I didn't have Twinkie's fat cheeks to squeeze every day. But now I have to deal with this new situation. Why didn't Mrs. Bosco ask *me* if I wanted another foster sister? Nobody ever asks me anything!

Dorinda Gets a Groove

I heave a deep sigh and walk into the living room. My foster brothers Nestor and Khalil are helping Mrs. Bosco fold the laundry. One good thing about Mrs. Bosco is, she makes the boys do as much housework as the girls, or they don't get to go outside and play.

Mr. Bosco is sitting on the end of the couch that isn't covered with clothes. I wonder why he isn't at work, even though he is wearing his security-guard uniform.

"Hi, Mr. Bosco," I say, trying to act normal. See, I'm not used to seeing him that much, because he's either working, sleeping, or hanging out at the Lenox Café down the block, where he can smoke his cigarettes in peace. Mr. Bosco isn't allowed to smoke in the living room, and sometimes I hear Mrs. Bosco fussing with him to clean the butts out of the ashtray in their bedroom.

"Oh, you got yourself a nice bag for school," Mr. Bosco says to me as I drop my cheetah backpack on the floor.

"Yeah," I reply. "Ms. Dorothea, um, the manager of the Cheetah Girls, gave it to me." I already told him where I got it, but I know he has a lot of stuff on his mind.

I wish Mr. Bosco would keep talking, so I could avoid dealing with the situation at hand, but he's gone back to watching TV.

"See the new butterfly I made?" Twinkie says to Mr. Bosco, holding up a butterfly she cut out of paper. She loves butterflies more than anything.

"That's nice—lemme see that," he says, and Twinkie moves closer.

I wish I could fly a million miles away, like one of Twinkie's butterflies. Without seeming obvious, I glance over at the new girl. She is sitting frozen like an angry statue on the faded orange couch. Her pretty face is covered with dried tears, and her eyebrows are squinched into a scowl. She is a real pretty caramel color, and I can tell, even though it's kinda dark in the living room, that her skin is smooth, and she doesn't have any scars on her face. She looks well taken care of—unlike Kenya. When Kenya first came here, her whole face was covered with white spots and scabs. The doctor said it was from a vitamin deficiency.

Suddenly I realize I'm staring, so I look away, just as part of the chocolate-chip cookie the new girl is holding in her hand drops on the floor.

"She doesn't want the cookie—I'll take it!"

volunteers Kenya, trying to take the rest of the cookie out of the girl's hand. The girl lets out a piercing scream.

"Kenya, I've told you to please leave her alone!" Mrs. Bosco snaps in her gruff, cracked voice.

I go over and pick the cookie crumbs off the floor, right by the girl's legs. Looking up at her, I smile and say, "Hi."

But she doesn't respond. She sits like a stone, and stares at me with her big, black, intense eyes, which are filled with so many feelings that it almost scares me.

"Dorinda, can you come in the kitchen for a second?" Mrs. Bosco says suddenly, getting out of her chair and picking up a pile of kitchen towels.

"Okay," I say, following her into the kitchen, and waiting to hear what she has to say.

"Gaye is going to be staying with us for—I don't know how long," Mrs. Bosco starts in, stuffing the hand towels into the kitchen drawer. Then she pauses, like she's uncomfortable. "So I guess you got yourself a new sister."

I don't want another sister! I shriek inside, but I hear myself say, "Okay."

"They found her wandering around in

Coney Island," Mrs. Bosco continues. "Nobody seems to know how she got there, or nothing. I know we don't have the room, but we'll just have to make do."

"Ms. Keisha says somebody saw her—um, *Gaye*—on the news," I tell her.

"Well, she's probably right, 'cuz if anybody knows everybody's business, it's Ms. Keisha."

Suddenly, I feel so sad for little Gaye. I remember when a strange lady came and took me from Mrs. Parkay's house—the first home I remember—without telling me why.

"I'll see you soon," Mrs. Parkay said to me, and waved good-bye. Even though I was only five, I remember thinking she was lying, because she had packed up all my clothes and handed them to the lady, who told me to get into her car. I remember asking the lady why my foster sister Jazmine wasn't coming with us. Now I know why, of course—Mrs. Parkay gave me away, and Jazmine wasn't my real sister—but someone named Tiffany is!

My legs feel weak, like spaghetti—so I sit down at the kitchen table.

"Are you okay, Dorinda?" Mrs. Bosco asks me.

"Yeah, I'm okay. How come Mr. Bosco didn't

go to work?" I ask, curious.

"Oh, he wanted to help out with Gaye and all. She was carrying on like a hurricane." Mrs. Bosco wipes her forehead with a tissue. "But she done settled down now, so he's gonna go to work late."

Suddenly I feel tears trickling down my cheeks. Mrs. Bosco is silent, then tells me, "Dorinda, we'll get through. She'll be all right. We'll *all* be all right."

"Yeah," I reply, wiping away the tears.

I sure hope so. But I can't help thinking of my half sister Tiffany, who was lucky enough to get adopted, and by rich folks, at that. Why do some people have all the luck, and others —like me and Gaye—have none?

Chapter 3

Going to school in the morning is a big production in my house on a *normal* day. But today, everybody is on edge, because our new foster sister Gaye stayed up the whole night crying. She is sitting at the table, staring at her breakfast, and I don't think there is much hope of getting her to eat it.

"Here," Mrs. Bosco says, placing a bowl of ice cream in front of her. It reminds me that Mrs. Bosco gave me ice cream the first day I came to live here, too.

At first, Gaye just stares at the bowl. Then, slowly, she picks up her spoon and starts fiddling with it. Finally, she starts wolfing down spoonfuls of ice cream.

"Why can't I have some?" Kenya asks, moaning like a big baby.

"No, Kenya. Can ya just eat your breakfast?" Mrs. Bosco snaps.

"Kenya, can ya please just shut up!" snipes Nestor.

"That's enough, Nestor," Mrs. Bosco says, then stands over Kenya. "I found some candy wrappers in your pants pocket when I was doing the laundry. Keep it up and you won't have a tooth left in your—"

Mrs. Bosco stops talking because the phone is ringing. Maybe someone from the agency is calling, because they found out more about Gaye's mother or something.

"Yes! Hi, Tiffany," Mrs. Bosco says warmly into the receiver.

Oh, no, not Tiffany! Why is she calling here before school?

"Yes, you just caught her," Mrs. Bosco says. "Uh-huh. Uh-huh. She's gotta leave by seven-fifteen to get to school on time—you know, with the trains and all. Uh-huh. Uh-huh. Uh-huh."

What is Tiffany gonna do, talk Mrs. Bosco's ear off? Finally, Mrs. Bosco hands me the receiver, even though I wish I could do a Houdini and disappear.

"Hi, Dorinda—remember me?" Tiffany asks, then lets out a nervous giggle.

"Of course I remember you," I respond, even though I can hear how stupid it sounds. I wonder if Tiffany's parents know she's running up their phone bill. They probably wouldn't care, with all the money they have.

"Well, I hadn't heard from you, so I thought I would give you a call. What's the deal-io?" Tiffany asks, giggling again.

"Um, nothing," I say, noticing that Tiffany is trying to talk like me.

"Um, I was wondering if you wanted to meet today after school?"

"Well, I'm not sure—I have to check and see if we have rehearsal today—you know, my group, the Cheetah Girls." I turn to see if Mrs. Bosco is within earshot, and she is—so I turn my back to her quickly.

"Um, I've gotta go to school now, so I can meet Chanel and Galleria," I say, hoping Tiffany will get off the phone.

"Oh, okay—so, you'll let me know if you can come over after school?" Tiffany is like a dog with a bone who won't leave it alone.

"Come over?" I ask, surprised.

"Yeah—my parents won't be here, and we can just hang out. 'Member I told you I wanted you to play my new keyboard?" Tiffany says, like she's dangling a carrot.

"Um, I don't know how to play keyboard," I say, unsure.

"It's fun—I'll show you," Tiffany says, not taking no for an answer.

"Um—I'll call you later and let you know."

After I hang up the phone, I wolf down the rest of my cereal, but Mrs. Bosco is staring at me. "You know, it's one thing when family leaves you, but it's another when they *find* you. You don't look a gift horse in the mouth, Dorinda— just check to make sure it has hooves."

I'm sure this is another one of Mrs. Bosco's Southern expressions. Thanks to her and the twins, I know a lot of them now—except for this one.

"I didn't say I wasn't going to see her," I protest, wiping the milk from the corner of my mouth with a paper napkin.

"I heard you tell that poor child that you have rehearsal. How you gonna rehearse when one of you has lost a hoof?" Mrs. Bosco snaps.

I chuckle involuntarily. Mrs. Bosco is funny sometimes, and she doesn't even know it. Now I feel stupid for telling a lie in front of her.

My brother Topwe drops his bowl on the floor, and I'm so relieved for the distraction. "I'll get it."

Topwe coughs, spitting a mouthful of cereal onto the table.

"Cover your mouth next time," Mrs. Bosco says softly.

"His cough doesn't sound good," I say, concerned. Topwe was born HIV-positive. Now he's seven, but he still gets bad colds sometimes.

"I'm gonna keep him home from school today," Mrs. Bosco says, like she has just decided it. "Dorinda, before you leave, get me the number for his school."

I dial the number for Mrs. Bosco and hand her the phone instead. This way I can leave without talking any more about Tiffany.

When I open the door downstairs in the lobby, I accidentally step in something really mushy and disgusting, that almost makes me slip. Someone has taken the garbage out of the cans and strewn it all over the courtyard—

again. During the night, a lot of homeless people tear open the garbage bags that sit tied and ready for collection.

Once I close the door, I notice that our super, Mr. Hammer, is behind the railing trying to clean up some of the strewn garbage.

"We're gonna get another ticket from the Sanitation Department," Mr. Hammer says gruffly, shaking his head in disgust. "I don't know why they don't just take the cans and sell them, instead of going through all the garbage and making this mess. Say, how's that computer working, Dorinda?" Mr. Hammer yells after me.

"Still clicking!" I say, smiling back. Last year, right after Christmas, someone threw out this really good computer, and Mr. Hammer fixed it up and gave it to me. It makes doing my homework a lot easier, and now I can talk to my crew on the Internet, you know what I'm saying? That reminds me, I was supposed to go online last night and say good night to Chanel, but I forgot, with all the drama going on in my house.

The trains are running on time—which is good, because I want to get to school early, so I can help Chanel if she needs it. Today is her first day back at school since her accident, and she may have a hard time getting around.

When I finally get to school, I head for the lockers, where I meet my crew before homeroom. A whole bunch of people are there, crowded around Chanel. I should have known she would be milking her crutches for points. She smiles at me like she's in a beauty contest, and stands there posing by the lockers, like she's holding a pair of designer crutches or something.

"Hey, wazzup?" I say to Galleria, since Chanel is busy holding court.

Before Galleria even says hello, she shoves a newspaper right in my face. "My mom saved this for us from the newspaper, so we could see it when we got back from Houston," she says, smirking.

My stomach flutters as I read the article with Galleria. Chanel stops holding court to join us, and balances herself by leaning on my shoulder. I read the article out loud, while Galleria looks over one of my shoulders and Chanel leans on the other one:

"'A copyright infringement suit was filed in L.A. on November 15 against pop star Kahlua Alexander, 19, by songwriter Mon' E Richardz.

Richardz claims that Alexander's song "Plucked by Def Duck" borrows too heavily from one of his own, "Goose on the Loose," recorded by In the Dark on 1999's *Struck by a Monkey Cane*. The lawsuit claims Alexander wrongfully gave songwriting credit to herself and producer Mouse Almighty, a.k.a. Sean Johnson. Richardz seeks undisclosed damages. Alexander's publicist contends, "Several musicologists have stated there is no copyright infringement. Kahlua, Mon' E, and Def Duck Records did not copy the song."'"

"Wow—a musicologist. That sounds deep, right?" Galleria riffs. "See, this goes to show it's not so easy to call something copyright infringement right out of the box."

"What does 'undisclosed damages' mean?" I ask, still staring at the article.

"A lot of duckets in the bucket, that's for sure," Galleria says, like she's an expert. "That's what my mom says. I bet Mon' E Richardz would probably settle for whatever royalty juice he could squeeze out of Kahlua's songwriting oranges, huh?"

"I guess," I say, not really sure.

"Mom says a lot of artists fight over this all

the time. But it costs a lot of money to sue somebody, because then you've got to prove that they stole your flavor." Galleria ponders for a moment. "I guess it wouldn't hurt if we tried to write original songs in the future, though."

Wow—that's the first time I heard Galleria say "we." I wonder if she means that she and Chanel will be writing another song together. Not that I'm asking, okay?

"Then again, being in the studio with Mouse Almighty singing *anybody's* songs would be like music to my ears," Galleria says, heaving a deep sigh.

"I hear that," I moan. "I wish we could start rehearsing again."

"*I* wish we could go to Mariah Carey's concert tomorrow," Chanel moans.

"Well, we don't have Mariah Carey money for the tickets—I mean, fifty duckets in the bucket is kinda steep, *mamacita*," Galleria counters.

"I hear that," I moan again. "I'd love to go to see Mariah Carey, too, you know what I'm saying? But I'm not paying!"

We crack up, and help Chanel go upstairs to her homeroom. Galleria and Chanel are in the same homeroom class, since they both major in Fashion Merchandising. I major in Fashion Design, so I have to go to the fourth floor by myself.

"How come you didn't log on to the chat room last night?" Chuchie asks me, still hanging on my shoulder.

"I couldn't," I answer softly. I guess it's time to tell my crew about Gaye. I take a deep breath, and tell them everything that's happened so far.

"You mean someone just left her by herself in the *street*?" Chanel asks in disbelief.

"Yeah—I guess so," I say, shrugging my shoulders. "Mrs. Bosco says the police have put up flyers all around Coney Island, where she was found, but nobody has come forward with any information."

Chanel gets tears in her eyes, so I pull out a tissue, just in case she needs it.

Galleria puts out her hand and does the Cheetah Girls handshake with me, but she seems dazed and confused, too. "Maybe someone will come and get her. If not, maybe *we* can figure something out."

"Maybe." I part ways with my crew. Taking the stairway up to the fourth floor, I think about what Galleria said. If anyone could track down a missing person, it would definitely be Bubbles. I mean, when the twins' uncle Skeeter was missing while we were in Houston, *she's* the one who figured out how to find him—or else he might have stayed missing for a whole lot longer. Maybe we *could* find Gaye's mother. On the other hand, what's the use of finding a mother who doesn't want her?

By the time I get to my last class of the day— sociology—I've forgotten all about my problems at home. That is, until the teacher, Mrs. Garber, tells us our class project: "Although most of you were born in this country, you'll discover that many of your great-grandparents, or even your grandparents, weren't. I want you to create a time line for one of your parents, tracing their origins, and making them parallel whatever historical events were happening in this country at the time. You don't have to account for every year of your parent's life, but most of them." Mrs. Garber draws a diagram of a time line on the board, and puts years next to the lines on the graph.

I can't do this! I want to yell. *I don't even know*

where my parents are! I don't even know who they are!

Mrs. Garber isn't finished giving me a headache. "After the time line, I want you to write an essay about your parent's migration pattern—describing in detail why they moved, what city in the United States they moved to, and what year. Don't go overboard, giving every detail of your parent's life. For example, we don't want to know what your mother ate for breakfast on the day you were born, okay?"

Some of the students in the class laugh at Mrs. Garber's joke. I just want to cry. I'll bet they know what their mother had for breakfast on the day they were born. I don't even know *where* I was born. Sinking into my chair, I just wish I could do a Houdini and disappear on the spot. How am I supposed to find out all this stuff, huh? By snapping my fingers?

"The migration essay should only be about three to four typewritten pages," Mrs. Garber continues. "We're not looking for *Roots*. Just have fun with it. If you do this assignment properly, you'll get a greater sense of the history that's living right under your noses. Everyone understand?"

I stare at Mrs. Garber's bright red blazer until

it becomes a blur. What am I going to do? I decide to wait until after everyone leaves the classroom, then talk to Mrs. Garber on the D.D.L. I would be embarrassed if anybody overheard my conversation, you know what I'm saying?

"Um, Mrs. Garber, can I speak to you?" I finally ask, my voice cracking.

"Yes, Dorinda, I'll be right with you," she says, scribbling something on some papers, then closing her folder. She looks me straight in the face, and asks, "Are you having trouble understanding the assignment for the class project?"

"Um, yeah. I, um, don't know how I'm going to do it," I say, shaking my head.

"Why not?" she asks.

"I don't, um, know much about my parents, so I don't know how I'm gonna complete—I mean—even *do* the project." I hope Mrs. Garber will get the drift without me having to spell it out.

"Who do you live with?" Mrs. Garber asks, concerned.

Now I guess I do have to tell her. "My foster parents," I say, and I feel myself getting embarrassed again.

"Okay—well then, ask one of your foster

parents if you can do a time line on one of them," Mrs. Garber says cheerfully.

I just stand there like a statue, so I guess Mrs. Garber figures something is still wrong—and it is. I don't want to ask Mrs. or Mr. Bosco so much stuff about their business. If they wanted me to know, they would have told me. I don't really know that much about them, except that Mrs. Bosco was born in North Carolina, and her grandfather worked as a tobacco sharecropper.

"I understand what you're going through, Dorinda," Mrs. Garber says, putting her arm on my shoulder.

Yeah, that's what a lot of people tell me so I don't feel bad, but they don't really understand what I'm going through.

"My grandparents were killed in the Holocaust, like many other Jews. After the war, many kids were placed in foster homes— including my mother," Mrs. Garber says, putting her arm around me.

"Really?" I ask, surprised. I guess she *does* understand—a little.

"There are so many stories in my family tree that are missing, that I would never be able to complete this assignment either. Do the best you can, Dorinda," Mrs. Garber tells me.

"Um—did they kill a lot of Jewish people in the Holo—"

"The Holocaust? Yes. Millions were killed, but the human spirit cannot be stopped. I think tragedy makes you appreciate the people in your life—the ones who really do care about you. I'm sure your foster mother will be happy to provide you with enough information for your time line."

"Thanks, Mrs. Garber," I say, then walk downstairs to meet my crew. Without even thinking, I go instead to the telephone booths by the cafeteria, and call my half sister Tiffany. "Um, you still want me to come over?"

"Yeah!" Tiffany responds, sounding really excited to hear my voice.

Walking toward the school exit, I take a deep breath, and find myself smiling. Mrs. Bosco was right. I shouldn't look a gift horse in the mouth—but I *am* gonna check to see if Tiffany has hooves!

Chapter 4

To get to Tiffany's house, on Eighty-second Street off Park Avenue, I have to take two trains, then walk. I can't believe all the kids I see walking around in private-school uniforms—they look like they're in an army or something, except for all the giggling. And the uniforms are all different, too—plaid and solid, gray, red, blue, navy—which means there are a lot of private schools in this neighborhood. I can tell some of the girls are rolling up their skirts at the waistband on the sneak tip, because their skirts look a little too short around their knobby knees, if you know what I'm saying. And some of the boys have mad funny haircuts, too.

Even with all the gangs of kids walking

around, it's a lot quieter in this neighborhood than mine. I can even hear some birds chirping. I open the door to Tiffany's building, but a doorman wearing white gloves beats me to it. Wow, I've never been in a building with a doorman! His uniform is green, with black and gold trim. He's wearing a hat with trim around it, too. I get a little nervous, and straighten my back so I seem taller—which is still a *lot* shorter than the doorman.

I feel strange asking for Tiffany Twitty, but I guess the doorman must be used to hearing her funny last name by now. He just asks for my name, without cracking a smile.

"Miss Rogers," I say, being polite, and standing aside so people can walk by me. See, Tiffany's real name, before she got adopted by the Twittys, was Karina Farber. That's what she told me, anyway. She said she found a baby picture of herself, that her parents kept in a locked safety box, and that her real name was written on the back. Tiffany seems like a supa sleuth, even if it took her eleven years to figure out she was adopted—which was something the Twittys didn't want her to know.

The doorman rings Tiffany's apartment, then

directs me to a bank of gilded elevators. They even have furniture in the lobby—a big burgundy couch, chairs, and a statue spouting water! Wow, I knew her parents were rich, but I didn't know Tiffany had it like *that*!

When the elevator door opens, there's already a lady inside, with a little white poodle. I don't mean to stare at the lady, but the beady eyes on the head of the fox stole around her neck are staring right at me! Then her dog sniffs at my legs, and suddenly I get embarrassed. The lady sees the look on my face, then asks me, "Do you have a dog?"

"No."

"Oh. Well, he's sniffing at something."

Oh, no. Maybe he's sniffing at the garbage from the courtyard of our building that I stepped in this morning! Suddenly I feel really dirty. I wonder if it's such a good idea that I came here. Maybe Tiffany's parents don't know I'm coming over, and they wouldn't like it if they found out.

"Come on, Baubles, let's go," the lady says, pulling her dog's shiny leash. I wonder if those are diamonds. Nah, they're probably rhinestones. The lady doesn't say good-bye to me when she gets out of the elevator. So I shout after her, "Have a nice day."

"Oh—yes, you too, dear," the startled lady says, turning around abruptly.

When Tiffany opens her apartment door, I greet her the same way. "Hello, dear!"

"Wazzup with you?" Tiffany says, her big blue eyes brightening when she sees me. I wonder why she's talking differently than when I first met her in Central Park. She's even wearing a cheetah turtleneck over her gray sweatpants.

"Check out your spots," I say, chuckling. I think Tiffany needs a little fashion coordination, but I don't want to hurt her feelings. "I met one of your neighbors in the elevator," I say, leaving the fashion bone alone for a sec.

"Who?"

"This, um, foxy lady with a white poodle," I say, then start to laugh. Whenever I get around Tiffany, I seem to get a case of the giggles.

"Oh, Mrs. Chirpy," Tiffany says, covering her mouth.

"That's not her *real* name!"

"Yes, it is! Her husband owns Chirpy Cheapies catalog, and her dog, Baubles, has bad breath."

Now I double over laughing, wondering how Tiffany makes up all these tall tales she tells. "How do you know he has bad breath—did you kiss him?"

"No!" Tiffany says, falling into me. "One day, this lady with a German shepherd got into the elevator, and Baubles went to kiss him, and the German shepherd barked."

"How do you know it wasn't a her?" I challenge her.

"Who?"

"The German shepherd—maybe it was a girl?"

"Maybe—but she sure didn't like Baubles sniffing her butt, 'cuz she whacked Baubles in the face with her big black tail!" Tiffany giggles, then plops down on the couch, sticking her shoeless feet under her.

We could never do that at my house—even though both the couches are so raggedy, Mrs. Bosco says she doesn't want them to get more messed up than they already are. "You stay home by yourself?" I ask.

"Yeah," Tiffany says, but when she hears a noise down the hallway, she quickly adds, "sometimes—when my brother isn't here."

"Oh," I say, 'cuz I don't want her to feel bad for exaggerating.

"He's in tenth grade—his name is Eric the Ferret."

I wonder if Tiffany's brother is adopted, like she is, but I decide it would be rude to ask, so I don't. Looking around the living room, I notice there are lots of Lucite boxes with dead butterflies hanging on the walls. "I wish Twinkie could see those," I say.

"Oh, those are my father's. Wanna see the pictures from Thanksgiving?" Tiffany asks excitedly.

"Yeah," I say, then put my backpack down on the carpet. Looking around at all the beautiful furniture and flowers in vases, I exclaim, "Wow, your house is nice." The living room almost looks like it's out of a magazine or something. They probably have a maid who comes in to clean the house every day.

Tiffany proudly hands me a stack of photos. In the first one, she is standing outside of a log cabin with her parents, and a tall boy with blond hair and big white teeth.

"That's Eric the Ferret—see, his teeth are really big."

"Oh. Where is this at?"

"It's our house in Massachusetts. We go there on weekends, and Thanksgiving and Christmas, too. In the summer it's cool, because there is a big lake to go swimming in."

"Well . . . I got to go to Houston for Thanksgiving."

"Really?" Tiffany acts like she's really interested, so I tell her all about the Cheetah Girls' adventures in H'Town—leaving out the showdown at the Okie-Dokie Corral, of course—with those fake wanna-be Cash Money Girls, who tried to run us out of Dodge over some stupid beef jerky.

"You got any pictures?" Tiffany asks excitedly.

"We bought a cheetah photo album when we were there, and now I'm gonna keep all the pictures we take," I announce proudly. Then I realize she wants to see them now. "Um, but I didn't bring it with me."

"Oh," Tiffany says, disappointed.

I tell Tiffany about the mouse in the kosher restaurant. She breaks out in a fit of giggles. "Oooo!" she squeaks, her eyes lighting up. "You wanna see my hamster, Miggy? He's in my bedroom."

Tiffany's bedroom is just like I expected it to be—frilly, pink, and filled with stuffed animals, CDs, and posters of singers—everybody from Mariah Carey to Kahlua Alexander to Limp Bizkit.

"Oh—you like Kahlua?" I ask, standing in front of the big poster of my favorite singer. Kahlua is responsible for the Cheetah Girls getting the hookup with Def Duck Records—even though nothing has happened yet. I explain this all to Tiffany, almost knocking into her fancy scooter, which is propped up against the wall.

"I wish I could put my hair in braids like Kahlua's," she says.

"She doesn't have braids anymore," I tell her. "We met her at Churl It's You! salon when she was getting her hair done for this movie."

"Really?" Tiffany asks, impressed. "But I like her hair better with braids." Tiffany smooths down her fine, blond hair, then adds, "My hair is more like Mariah's when she straightens it."

"You like Mariah, too." I smile.

"Are you kidding? I want to see her in concert this Friday, but my parents won't let me go," Tiffany says, annoyed.

I wonder why they won't. I'll bet they could

afford the fifty dollars for the cheapest tickets. Maybe they think she's too young or something.

"Is the record company really going to let you go in the studio and record songs?" Tiffany asks excitedly.

"I guess—they said they would team us with producer Mouse Almighty—you know, he worked on Karma's Children, Kahlua, and Sista Fudge's records, too."

"Really?" Tiffany asks with bugged eyes. Every time I tell her anything about the Cheetah Girls, she acts like a kid in a candy store. Soon I get to hear why.

"I want to be a singer too," she confesses, kind of self-consciously.

"Let me hear you sing," I say, egging her on so I can see if she has the skills to pay the bills.

"Not now," she says, getting all coy and blushing. She walks over to a pink trunk in the corner of the room and says, "See? Look in my glamor trunk. I was a Cheetah Girl, too—even when I was little." Holding up a tiny cheetah skirt with a matching cape, Tiffany puts it against herself and wiggles her hips. "I used to walk around the house wearing this outfit, and singing like Mariah Carey—'I'm just your but-terfly, baby!'"

I chuckle at Tiffany's squeaky voice.

"I'm just playing around—but I really do sing. When I know you better, I'll do it," she says shyly, then takes her pet hamster out of her cage. "Want to pet Miggy?"

"Okay," I say, letting Tiffany put the hamster in my palm. I keep looking around Tiffany's room, until I notice the electronic keyboard against the wall.

"That's the keyboard I got for my birthday," she brags. "My parents felt so bad about me finding out I was adopted, they let me have it. Now they're being really nice to me."

"They weren't mad at you for snooping around and finding the key to the locked box?"

"Nope—they felt too guilty about the whole thing," Tiffany says, lying back on her bed. Then her face gets sad. "I told Christine, my best friend at school, that I found out I was adopted, and she went and told Leandra, who hates me. Then Leandra went and told every-body at school. Now the kids are making fun of me. They call me an adopted Miss Piggy."

Tiffany is—well, chubby—but that sounds

really mean. I think she's kinda cute. Now I start thinking about the situation I've got at home. "I got a new foster sister yesterday."

"Really?"

"Yeah—this girl that was on the news, because her mother left her by herself in Coney Island." Suddenly, I feel uncomfortable. Why am I telling her this?

Tiffany sits up straight on the bed and stares at me. "How old is she?"

"Nobody knows. She looks about five, I guess. We don't know anything about her, except she says her name is Gaye."

"That's so sad," Tiffany responds. "Maybe somebody will come looking for her."

"Maybe—they had her picture on the news and everything. I guess somebody has to know her, right?"

"Unless she's not from New York," Tiffany says, like a divette detective.

"Wow, I never even thought of that," I say.

"Maybe her mother came all the way to New York so nobody would know her, and then left her there in Coney Island, because she knew somebody would find her," Tiffany says, her blue eyes widening.

Maybe Tiffany knows where *I* was born, I'm thinking—but I don't want to ask her. "You said you were born in California?" I ask instead, hoping maybe she'll tell me more.

"Yeah—I think our mother moved there, then left me—I mean us." Tiffany doesn't seem sad about it at all. "Where were you born?"

"I don't know," I say, disappointed that *she* doesn't know. "I guess I always thought I was born in New York, but now I'm not so sure." Suddenly, I get a pain in my chest. "I don't care where I was born," I blurt out. "I don't care where our mother is!"

"*I* do," Tiffany says. "Maybe we can find her together."

"You can go look for her yourself—because I have better things to do with my time!" I pout.

"Okay," Tiffany says, shrugging her shoulders. Then she gets up, grabs a booklet, and hands it to me. "Here's the book for the keyboard. You wanna learn how to play it?"

"Yeah. Why not—if you don't mind listening to some wack playing!"

Chapter 5

I have never played any instrument before, so I feel kind of nervous about playing the keyboard—with Tiffany, no less. But it turns out she is a really good teacher. After an hour of trying, I'm actually playing pieces of songs I know. *I can't believe I'm learning to play the keyboard!* "This is dope," I say after a while. "Let me hear *you* play something."

Tiffany starts playing, and I recognize the song instantly. Kahlua Alexander and Mo' Money Monique's duet, "The Toyz Is Mine."

Tiffany definitely has mad skills playing the keyboard. Next to me, she sounds stomping. "I'm going to get us some lemonade and cookies," Tiffany says, jumping up.

I bang around some more on the keys, and I

feel like I could do this all day. Then I feel a lump rising in my throat. I wonder how much a keyboard like this costs?

"Um, where did your parents buy the keyboard at?" I ask Tiffany when she comes back, handing me a pretty pink glass of lemonade.

"Kmart. It cost twelve hundred dollars," she says matter-of-factly.

"How do you know what your birthday present costs?" I ask, surprised.

"'Cuz when we went to Kmart to buy my school supplies, I went into the aisle where the keyboards were and I saw mine—that's how," Tiffany has that satisfied smirk on her face—the one she gets when her supa-sleuth skills pay off.

"It's going to be a long way down the yellow brick road before I can afford a keyboard," I moan. Then I start wondering why I should bother learning at all, if I'm not going to be able to afford one.

"You can come over and play it whenever you want, Dorinda," Tiffany says, putting her hand on my shoulder.

Then she goes on teaching me the keyboard like nothing happened. I get interested again, and soon I forget about whether I can afford to buy one of my own. At least when I do get one,

I'll know how to play it. "You know, you'd make a really good teacher," I tell her.

"Are you trying to tell me I'm not going to be a singer?" Tiffany says, turning to me on the bench, and giving me that earnest look with her big, blue eyes.

"I didn't say that," I respond, my cheeks turning warm.

All of sudden, Tiffany breaks out into a big smile. "Psych! I know I'm gonna be a singer, too."

I don't want to rain on Tiffany's parade, you know what I'm saying? Who am I to say she can't be a singer, even if she sounds like a hoarse hyena in a rainstorm?

"Maybe I could sing for the rest of the Cheetah Girls, and they'll let me be in the group with you!" Tiffany says, getting excited and putting her head on my shoulder. Her blond hair is so soft, and I smell the familiar baby powder scent that now reminds me of her.

"I don't know, Tiffany. It's not my group or anything," I say, because I feel bad. Here she is being nice to me, trying to be my sister and everything, and I don't want to be down with her like that.

"Please?" she says, giving me a pleading

look with her big, blue eyes. Now I can tell she's really serious. "I could sing and play the keyboard. I mean, you don't have a keyboard player, right?" I'll bet she's used to getting her way about everything.

"Well, we don't use instruments at all—you know that; you came and saw us at the Apollo, when we were in the 'Battle of the Divettes' competition. See, we use tracks, just like a lot of other groups do. It costs a lot of money to have live musicians onstage."

"I'd play the keyboard for free," Tiffany says, not letting up.

"Well, I'll ask the rest of the Cheetah Girls if you can sing for them. How's that?" I say, finally giving in, and hoping she'll leave the Cheetah Girls bone alone for a while.

"Okay—when?" Tiffany asks directly.

"I . . . have to call and ask them."

"You can call Galleria now," Tiffany suggests, handing me the phone. "She's the leader of the group, right?"

"R-right," I say, then add quickly, "but she's not home right now."

"Do the Cheetah Girls go into a chat room?" Tiffany asks, like she's getting at something.

I can't tell her what chat room we go into—then maybe she'll be trying to sweat us all the time! But how can I *not* tell her? "Um . . . Yeah."

"Well, which one?"

"Phat Planet," I say, telling her the truth, because I don't want to lie.

"My onscreen name is LimpCutie," Tiffany says, proud of herself.

I realize that it's probably a riff off of Limp Bizkit, seeing as she's got their poster on her wall.

"I can go on tonight, and see if the Cheetah Girls are in there, okay?"

I know she isn't really asking me, so I don't say anything. Tiffany walks over to her closet and opens a trunk. "Here's the safety equipment I told you I was gonna give you," she says, pulling out a pair of knee guards and a pair of elbow guards.

"Oh, that's okay," I say, suddenly feeling embarrassed again. I don't want her giving me things. I don't think it's cool.

"Take them—I told you when we first met in the park that I had an extra set. I don't need them." Tiffany shoves them into my lap.

"Okay," I say, smiling, "then I'm going to make you an outfit."

"Really?" Tiffany just gets excited about everything. Skating, singing, playing the keyboard, you name it!

"Yup, I'm gonna design an outfit and make it for you. Let me take your measurements," I say, finally feeling like I have something to give her, too. "I have a sewing machine at home."

"Really?" Tiffany says again. I guess that's the one thing she doesn't have. "I don't know how to sew anything."

"You got a tape measure?" I ask her, chuckling.

"No—wait. I think my mom has one in her room." Tiffany runs to get it.

All of a sudden, I hear the apartment door open, and some voices in the hallway. I get nervous, because I realize that it's probably her parents. I hope they don't get upset that I'm here. I can't make out what they're talking about, so I just get off the keyboard bench, and sit in the princess throne by Tiffany's bed.

Tiffany comes running back into the room and whispers, "I can't get the tape measure now, but we'll do it next time you come over. My mother's home from work, and she wants to say hello."

"Okay," I say.

Tiffany drags me by my arm back into the living room, where Mrs. Twitty is sitting on the couch, wearing a black dress with a strand of white pearls around her neck. She seems really nice and proper, just like she did when I met her at the Apollo.

"Hi," I say, smiling.

"Please sit down, Dorinda," motions Mrs. Twitty.

"Thank you. That was real nice of you, bringing Tiffany to see the Cheetah Girls at the Apollo."

"Oh, it was fun," Mrs. Twitty says. "I really enjoyed it. I think you girls are very good. You know, that's all Tiffany talks about now—being in a singing group. She just *loves* singing groups. She plays those CDs all the time, and she loves that keyboard," Mrs. Twitty says, like she's not sure if *she* likes it or not.

"I want to go to a performing arts school, like the Walker twins do," Tiffany says, putting her head on her mother's shoulder.

"Well, we won't have any of that, dear," Mrs. Twitty says. "We pay good money to send you to St. Agnes."

Tiffany pouts, and I can tell she's not happy,

but I'm not saying anything.

"Dorinda is gonna let me try out to be a Cheetah Girl!" Tiffany says suddenly.

I can't believe she said that! I didn't say she could try out for the Cheetah Girls! I decide I'd better keep my mouth shut, but Mrs. Twitty is definitely interested in hearing what I have to say about it.

"Is that right?" she asks, looking straight at me. Her eyes are really blue, just like Tiffany's. In a way, *she* looks like Tiffany's real mother, I guess—except that her hair is dark brown, and her nose is straighter than Tiffany's. "That would be really good for her."

I guess Mrs. Twitty sees the confused look on my face, because she quickly adds, "To try out, I mean."

"Yeah, um, I'm gonna ask the rest of the Cheetah Girls if she can," I say, glad that Mrs. Twitty has made it seem less scary than it is.

"I'm teaching Dorinda how to play my keyboard," Tiffany says, like she's really proud of herself. "She's really good, too!"

"Tiffany just loves that thing—she'd play it all day if we let her," Mrs. Twitty says, nodding her head at me.

I wonder if I should say good-bye, because I've been sitting here a long time. I'd better be getting uptown, to see what's cooking with my new foster sister, Gaye, if you know what I'm saying. Just thinking about going home, the heavy weight that I feel lately on my chest has come back in full force.

"The two of you sure have something in common," Mrs. Twitty continues.

"What?" I ask, suddenly realizing that I spaced out for a second.

"Well, you're both musically inclined. Tiffany plays the keyboard, and you sing. That's what I meant," Mrs. Twitty adds, like she hopes she didn't offend me or anything.

"Oh, yeah," I say, nodding. I don't think it's such a good idea for me to ask the Cheetah Girls if Tiffany can try out.

"That's all Tiffany talks about is singing. Or this singer and that singer. Did you see all the posters on her walls?"

"Yeah," I answer.

If you ask me, I think Tiffany is just trying to be in the mix 'cuz she thinks it's fun. I wonder what Tiffany sounds like when she's really singing. She seems kinda shy about singing in front of people—and Tiffany isn't shy other-wise, if you know what I'm saying.

"Would you like to stay for dinner?" Mrs. Twitty asks me.

"No, thank you," I respond quickly. I want to tell her why I have to go home, but I feel embarrassed, so I decide not to.

"I got out of work earlier today than usual," Mrs. Twitty continues, "so we won't have to eat takeout."

"Where do you work?" I ask Mrs. Twitty, since I figure I can talk about that.

"I'm the research director for The Butterfly Foundation," Mrs. Twitty says proudly.

"Oh—that's why you have all the butterflies on the wall," I say excitedly. "My fos—um, my sister Twinkie loves butterflies."

"Well, she'll have to visit sometime. My hus-band is the head scientist there—that's where we met, you know. I guess you could say the 'nutty professor' caught me in his net," she says chirpily.

"Wait till I tell Twinkie—she'll be so excited!" I say, chuckling at Mrs. Twitty's joke. She is a funny lady. "Well, I'd better get home." I get up and grab my backpack and the safety equipment. Suddenly, I feel self-conscious, like a bag lady or something. Mrs. Twitty notices me clutching the bag, so I quickly add, "Um, Tiffany gave me the pads—she said she didn't need them."

"Oh, yes, she must have outgrown those by now," Mrs. Twitty says, causing Tiffany to wince.

"Mom, I can still fit in them," she protests; but when Mrs. Twitty looks at her, she adds with a sheepish giggle, "Well, almost!"

I guess it *is* kinda weird that I'm smaller than Tiffany, even though I'm older.

"Well, I'm glad someone can put them to good use," Mrs. Twitty says, then gets up to show me to the door.

Once I'm in the hallway, Tiffany sticks her head out her door and says, "Sorry you have to bounce, *mamacita!*"

"Me, too," I say, chuckling at my sister. As I walk to the subway station, I'm thinking about how much fun I had learning the keyboard. Even though I'm jealous that she has so much and I have so little, I'm glad I came over to my sister Tiffany's house—she is a trip! Besides, she's my for real, forever sister—and that means a lot.

Chapter 6

Thank goodness for my crew. They may not live in foster homes, but I know they care about me. When I meet them at Riverside Church for our Kats and Kittys Klub meeting, I just start babbling about the latest drama in my house, when I didn't even plan on telling them diddly widdly.

Last night, Gaye kept me up all night, crying and screaming from nightmares. She even got out of bed and ran down the hallway, yelling that a car was chasing her. "Please don't hit me!" she kept screaming, over and over.

"Maybe she wasn't really talking about a car," Galleria says, putting her arm around my shoulders, and I can tell her mind is working on the divette detective tip.

"That is just so sad," Aqua says, and I see tears forming in her eyes. "I can't believe a mother would shame the Lord by leaving her child in the street."

I wonder where my mother left me, a voice shrieks in my head. It's something I've never thought about before, but now that Gaye is living with us, I can't get that thought out of my head. Not that I really want to know, if you know what I'm saying.

When we're climbing up the steps inside the church, Chanel almost misses one, and wobbles with her crutches into the railing, but luckily, Aqua grabs her arm. "Let me help you, Chanel," she insists.

Now I feel bad for babbling while poor Chanel is hobbling around on crutches. It seems like I'm always thinking about myself. Even though Chanel hasn't whined once about spraining her ankle, I know those crutches must be driving her loco.

"Stop it. I can help myself!" she snaps at Aqua, so I know I'm right. She must really be buggin', because Chanel is really sweet to everybody—maybe a little *too* sweet, if you know what I'm saying. See, Chanel doesn't always stand up for herself, but I guess Galleria stands up enough for both of them.

"What are we talking about tonight?" Angie asks her sister as we approach the landing. Once a month, we attend a general meeting for the Kats and Kittys Klub, this really dope social club for teens that Galleria and Chanel have belonged to since they were babies. The Kats and Kittys Klub has lots of chapters all around the country, and Aqua and Angie transferred into the metropolitan chapter when they moved to the Big Apple last summer. That was really lucky for us, because it's how we all hooked up and became the Cheetah Girls together.

"Let's see—our volunteer drive for Christmas," Aqua says. Aqua and Angie are teen advisors on the volunteer committee. Galleria and Chanel are on the party and events planning committee.

I'm just lucky they let me in the building, if you know what I'm saying. See, membership into the Kats and Kittys Klub is something like six hundred duckets a year, but Galleria and Chanel pulled a few strings so I could get a one-year scholarship for free. Actually, I think they pulled a whole ball of yarn, but just don't want me to know.

"We've also got to finish planning our Christmas bash, 'cuz the season is coming up, and we've gotta head down Candy Cane Lane with fortune and fame!"

"Don't remind me about Christmas," I snort. "I'm not so sure I want to be in my house at Christmastime this year."

Everyone gets silent for a second. Then Chanel asks, "What does your foster mother say about keeping Gaye?"

"That we are just gonna make do," I say, shrugging my shoulders. "I know she can't afford it, but I guess we'll get by."

"Do they give Mrs. Bosco money for that?" Aqua asks nervously.

"Yeah, but not much. Mrs. Bosco says that after she buys the milk and cereal, that check is long gone. I can forget about getting a keyboard, that's for sure. No way Mrs. Bosco can afford to buy me one. Do you know that a keyboard costs twelve hundred dollars?"

"What happened?" Chanel asks, puzzled.

Then I realize I should tell them about my

trip to Tiffany's crib. "My sister Tiffany is teaching me how to play her keyboard."

"We didn't know you went to see her," Galleria snorts.

"I didn't even know I was going to see her. I decided on a dime, right after last period yesterday."

"She knows how to play real good?" is all Aqua wants to know.

"Well, yeah," I respond. "She had a few grooves, but what do I know?"

I wonder if I should tell my crew that Tiffany wants to be in the group. No way, José! I decide.

As we make our way to the room where the Kats and Kittys meeting is held, Galleria heaves a deep sigh. "Well, I'd better brace myself for the Red Snapper trying to get his hooks into me again."

The Red Snapper—a.k.a. Derek Ulysses Hambone—is a student at our school, and he has a crush on Galleria. As soon as he found out she was a Kats and Kittys member, he went and joined, because he's got it like that. See, Derek's family are automotive "big Willies" in Detroit, who moved to the East Coast when his father expanded his thingamajig company—he manufactures some sort of widgets that you need to put in cars. I don't know much about cars, so I forgot the name of the part.

"I can't believe he joined," Chanel moans.

As we make our entrance, Mrs. Bugge, our chapter treasurer, gives us a shout-out: "Here come the Cheetah Girls. I guess we can start now." Everybody feels bad that Chanel is walking on crutches, so I think Mrs. Bugge is trying to blow up our spot, if you know what I'm saying.

The Kats and Kittys Klub in New York has two fund-raisers a year, so that we can donate duckets to charities. Today, we'll decide which organizations to donate the duckets to—and since Aqua and Angie are the teen advisers on that committee, they'll get to help in the voting process.

We all walk to the other end of the table, where there are empty seats. Derek bares his gold tooth as soon as he catches Galleria's eye. "Hey, wazzup, Cheetah Girl?" he says in his goofy voice. Derek is wearing a baseball cap turned backward, which makes his pinhead look even funnier.

Finally, Indigo Luther makes *her* entrance—

and I guess it would be hard to miss, considering the fact that she's six feet tall (even though she's only fourteen). The hot-pink rabbit jacket she's wearing would be hard to miss, too. Indigo Luther is our teen chapter president, and already a professional model. "Hi, everyone, sorry I'm late," she says, plopping her red rabbit pocketbook on the table like it's a trophy.

"Can I have your attention please," says Mrs. Bugge. She hands out the minutes from the last Kats and Kittys Klub meeting. "Here is our latest treasury report. We have to take a vote on which charity organizations we would like to donate money to. As you may remember, this is the money we raised from this year's Kats and Kittys Halloween Bash, where the Cheetah Girls performed for the very first time—but not the last."

Everyone applauds, and my crew and I look at each other, smiling with pride to think how far we've come, and how far we still have to go.

Mrs. Bugge clears her throat. "Aquanette and Anginette—could you take over the voting, please?"

"Our choices for donations are the Riverside Youth Fund, Pediatric Illness Fund, Sickle-Cell

Anemia Foundation," Aquanette starts in.

I wonder why she hasn't included an organization that helps foster kids. But since I'm not on the committee, it's not my place to say anything. Besides, I realize, the other organizations deserve the donations anyway.

"But what I would like to suggest," Aqua continues, "is that we consider donating the money to ACS, in the Division of Foster Care, for the specific use of the Bosco family. They're the family that has taken in the girl you may have seen on the news—the one named Gaye, who was found wandering around Coney Island and remanded into foster care."

Everyone gets real quiet, and I can feel some of the Kats and Kittys members staring at me. I stare down at the table like I'm looking for something, because I feel my ears burning with embarrassment. I can't *believe* Aquanette is saying this in front of the whole Kats and Kittys Klub! I'll bet they all already know that I live in a foster home, and that everybody's been talking about me behind my back. In fact, that must be how Galleria and Chanel got me a free membership!

I feel myself sinking lower into my chair. I can't even look at Aqua while she's talking.

"I think we should explain," Angie says, cutting in. "On Monday, Dorinda's foster mother, Mrs. Bosco, took Gaye in, after every effort was made to locate her mother, or anybody who knew her. Mrs. Bosco is already taking care of eleven foster children."

"Well, I think that's a very valid suggestion," Mrs. Bugge says. "Let's include it in our choices."

"Okay," Aqua says. "So we'll begin voting now. We'll pass around the ballots—please fill them out and return them to the basket."

All of a sudden, I feel Galleria's hand pressing down on mine. She must know how embarrassed I am. After everyone in the room finishes voting, Aqua and Angie separate the ballots into piles according to the votes marked on them, then Mrs. Bugge reads the final vote.

"For the record, this year's Kats and Kittys Klub charity donation will be sent to ACS, in the Division of Foster Care—to be allocated for the specific aid of Gaye, a foster child in the temporary custody of Mrs. Bosco." Mrs. Bugge smiles at me warmly.

All of a sudden, I burst into tears. I wish people wouldn't feel sorry for me all the time—it makes me feel totally humiliated!

I keep my head down. I can feel Galleria giving me a hug, before she gets up to speak as the teen adviser for the events planning committee. I'm relieved when she starts talking, because everybody isn't looking at me anymore.

"The time is upon us to nail down plans for our Christmas Eggnogger. Instead of throwing it at the Hound Club like we did last year, I would like to suggest that we try another place," Galleria says, like she's not taking no for an answer.

"Well, what do you suggest?" Indigo says, looking straight up at Galleria.

"We heard about this new club called the Weeping Willow," Galleria says, like she's daring Indigo to defy her.

"I know that place," Indigo says like she's bragging. "You haven't been there yet, have you?"

"No, um, Chanel and I thought we would check it out after we get the committee's approval."

"Well, when I modeled in a fashion show for Phat Farm, they threw a party there afterward. I don't think we can sell enough tickets to fill capacity—I mean, it's kinda big."

When I look up, I see the grimace on Galleria's face.

"If we get each nonsenior member to bring five guests, and senior members to bring ten, then I think we can fill and chill the club, you know what I'm saying?" Galleria asks, looking around at the other members for their opinion—including Derek's.

"Yeah!" Derek says, piping up in Galleria's defense. "And, um, are we going to invite peeps from other chapters? That could bring in the noise, you know what I'm saying?"

"That's basically up to us," Galleria retorts, waiting for Indigo to counter.

"I say we invite other chapters," Indigo agrees, surprising Galleria.

"And one parent from each chapter has to be a chaperone—no ifs or buts about it," Mrs. Bugge adds.

"Okay," Chanel pipes up, then giggles. "Can we go look at the place?"

"Agreed," says Indigo. "I move that we close the meeting, and that the advisers for the party committee report directly to me and Mrs. Bugge during the planning."

"I second!" yells Derek.

"I third that we head out of here and eat some steer," Aqua pipes up.

"That sounds finger-lickin' good to me," Galleria chuckles, happy that the meeting is over, and we can be by ourselves.

Of course, I know that Aqua is just saying we should go to McDonald's for a Big Mac. But even though I'm having a Mac attack myself, I don't want to hang with my crew right now, because they really embarrassed me. I need to figure out how I can get out of this plan, and head home to a can of Spam or something. . . .

Chapter 7

Mrs. Bosco is so happy about the Kats and Kittys Klub donation to ACS—the Administration of Children's Services—that she just dismisses my feelings about being called out as a foster child in front of my fellow Kats and Kittys. She makes me so mad, I don't want to ask if I can talk to her about her background for my school time-line project.

"Dorinda, sometimes I think you have a hard head. Your life is gonna be so much easier when you learn not to look a gift horse in the mouth." She is folding up the laundry—which it seems like she's doing all the time, because there are so many people living in our house.

"I know—and I'm supposed to check it, to

make sure it has hooves," I say, trying to go along with the program. I still don't know what Mrs. Bosco means by the last part, but I'm not gonna ask. I've had enough embarrassment for a whole year!

"I don't think God loves you any less than other children, just because you lost your mother," Mrs. Bosco continues. "And obviously, those Kats and Kittys children like you, too."

Now I feel stupid for coming home and crying in front of Mrs. Bosco. I didn't mean to, but sometimes I get so clogged up inside, everything spouts out all over the place—kinda like that girl in *The Exorcist*. I guess I don't know how to express my feelings the way other people do.

Suddenly, what Mrs. Bosco just said sinks in. What did she mean by "I lost my mother?" Maybe she knows what happened to her, and she's just not telling me. Maybe she's dead!

"Tiffany called you twice today," Mrs. Bosco says, shaking out Topwe's red corduroy pants, then folding them really carefully. I hear Topwe coughing from his bedroom. He went to bed early because he's still not feeling well—otherwise he would never miss his favorite television show, *She's All That and a Pussycat*.

At least I'm not HIV-positive like Topwe. My problems are nothing next to his, or Gaye's. So why am I being so self-conscious about everything?

"Maybe I should make him some warm milk and bring it to him in the bedroom?" I ask Mrs. Bosco, getting up to go to the kitchen.

"No, Dorinda. I gave him some cough syrup and his medicine before he went to bed. Let him sleep if he can." Mrs. Bosco looks up at me, adjusting her bifocal glasses. I know her eyesight isn't good, but sometimes I wonder if she does that because she wants to look closer inside me or something—like she has gamma-ray vision.

"Tiffany told me all about you learning the keyboard. You ain't said nothing about it." I can tell, by the tone in her voice, that she's really asking, "Wazzup with that?"

"Oh—yeah. It was a lot of fun," I respond, trying to sound kinda bubbly about it. "It's not easy or anything. I'd have to practice a lot—but I would like to learn it some more."

"Well, that sounds real good," Mrs. Bosco says. "'Member you used to want to play the piano?"

I wonder why Mrs. Bosco is bringing that up.

The only reason I never took piano lessons is because she couldn't afford it.

"Maybe Tiffany'll let you practice with her again. That'd be good for you two," she goes on.

I know I shouldn't feel disappointed, but I do when she doesn't say anything about buying me my own keyboard.

"She also said you might let her be in your group," Mrs. Bosco says, searching about the bottom of the basket for stray socks.

I can't believe Tiffany told Mrs. Bosco that! She's just not going to let up about being in the Cheetah Girls. "Let me help you with those," I say quickly. There's always a lot of socks, and sometimes it's hard to tell the blue ones from the brown ones or the black ones, especially since the light in the living room isn't really bright enough.

But Mrs. Bosco is staring at me, knowing that I'm avoiding answering her. "Well, it's not my group," I say, trying to explain. "And I didn't exactly tell Tiffany she could be in it."

Now I feel bad—again! After all, Tiffany let me practice on her keyboard. I guess the least I could do is ask the Cheetah Girls if she could audition, like she wants to. "I guess I could ask the

Cheetah Girls to hear her sing," I say, giving in.

"Well, that's all you can do, right?" she says, like she's finally going to leave me alone about it. "You know, if you keep your word, then the rest takes care of itself."

"Yes, I guess you're right," I say, folding the socks tightly into each other. Suddenly, I realize that I haven't heard one word from my new foster sister. "What's up with Gaye?" I ask.

"I guess she done finally wore herself out," Mrs. Bosco says with a heavy sigh.

"Have you, um, heard anything else?" I ask hesitantly. After what Galleria said, I'm beginning to wonder myself. Someone, somewhere, must know Gaye, or know someone who knows her.

"When people disappear, they usually don't want to be found, and they have a real good way of staying lost," Mrs. Bosco says.

From the way she looks at me, straight in the face, I suddenly realize that she *does* know something about my mother—I think she's trying to tell me that *my* mother disappeared, and doesn't want to be found.

Twinkie and the rest of the girls have finished with their baths. I can't believe that

Monie, my oldest foster sister, who is sixteen, actually gave them a bath and got them into their pajamas! Monie usually only thinks about herself.

Twinkie peeks into the living room, even though it's way past her bedtime. "Hi, Dorinda," she whispers.

"You can come on in for a second, Rita, but then you better go to bed," Mrs. Bosco says, smiling at her. "Come take y'all's clothes and put them in the drawer."

"Okay," Twinkie says, taking the folded clothes in her arms. "Dorinda, the Butterfly lady was on television."

"Oh, was she singing?" I ask Twinkie. Twinkie calls Mariah Carey the Butterfly lady, because it's the name of one of her hits.

"No," Twinkie says, "but I wish I could go see her sing!"

"I know, Twinkie, but her concert costs fifty dollars, and that's a lot of money," I say, giving her a hug.

"Fifty dollars?" Mrs. Bosco says, almost choking. "She'd better be doing a whole lot of singing for that kind of money! Where's she singing at?"

"Madison Square Garden," I add, feeling a twinge of sadness. Now that I'm in the Cheetah Girls, I spend a lot less time with Twinkie. We used to be so close. I wish I could take her to see Mariah Carey. Shoot, I can't wait till Twinkie can see me and the Cheetah Girls sing! "So what was she doing, Twinkie?"

"Oh, she was with a lot of kids, talking about foster children. Telling people to take foster children like us," Twinkie explains.

"Really?" I wonder what she's talking about.

"That's not what she means, Dorinda. She didn't say nothing about y'all or nothing. Just, it's some kinda, some new, um—"

"Program?" I ask.

"Uh, yeah," Mrs. Bosco says, then changes her mind. "No, it's not really a program, you know—it's more like a commercial, where she's trying to get people to take in foster children, and they tell you a number to call, you know."

"Oh. You mean like a public service announcement?"

"Yeah—that's exactly it," Mrs. Bosco says, finally satisfied.

"I haven't seen it," I say, surprised.

"See, Rita, when you get bigger, you gonna be

right smart like Dorinda. She don't miss a trick."

"How come she don't have us on television with her?" Twinkie asks me.

"Well, I guess—no, I *know* if she knew you, she would," I tell Twinkie. But what I really want to say is, "Why would you want to be on television, announcing to the world that you're a foster child?" I wouldn't do it, not even if Mariah Carey asked me herself, you know what I'm saying?

"Rita, there's a whole lot of kids like you in the world, and I guess she's trying to help, because she's famous and people will listen to her." Mrs. Bosco motions for Twinkie to come closer, so she can smooth down her hair. Twinkie's hair is always flying all over the place like a pinwheel or something. "If there were enough homes for foster kids, then she wouldn't have to ask people to take them in, but Lord knows those people running the agencies can barely tie their own shoelaces!"

Mrs. Bosco doesn't like dealing with the foster care agency, because she thinks they're kinda disorganized.

"If they paid those people enough money, then I'll bet they'd find homes for every child,"

Mrs. Bosco goes on, like she's just getting started. "They don't mind paying these people all kinds of money on television just to act stupid."

"Okay, Twinkie, it's time for bed," I say, kissing her good night. I decide not to tell her about Tiffany's parents and The Butterfly Foundation—yet. I don't want to get her hopes up, and then find out I can't really bring her there.

Now that Mrs. Bosco and I are alone, I ask her about doing the time-line project for my sociology class.

"Well," Mrs. Bosco chuckles, "I have a hard enough time remembering what happened yesterday, let alone forty years ago, but I guess I could try."

"Thank you, Mom," I say, because I know she likes me to call her that. "I'll probably start it next week."

"That'll be something telling you about all my kin—there's a whole lot of us still down in North Cadilakky," Mrs. Bosco chuckles, making fun of her home state, North Carolina. "Believe me when I tell you, when you have a little kin, you should pay some mind to keeping them around."

"Yeah," I say turning around and smiling

because I know what Mrs. Bosco is getting at—
that I should be happy my sister Tiffany found
me. Right now, though, I'd better at least see if
my crew is in the chat room, so I can ask them
about hearing Tiffany sing.

First I go into Rita's bedroom, to take a look
at Gaye. It's hard for me to imagine her sleeping, after all that drama she caused last night. I
tiptoe closer, and see her curled up in a ball,
with her thumb stuck in her mouth. She seems
kinda old to be doing that, but I guess that's all
she has that she can call her own. I wonder
what she likes—maybe she likes teddy bears,
like Arba does. Or butterflies, like Twinkie. Or
DIVA dolls, like Kenya. All of a sudden, I feel
excited about getting to know Gaye. Maybe it
won't be so bad having her here.

"Good night, Doreety," Twinkie says, imitat-
ing the way Arba says my name. Arba is from
Albania, and she has her own way of talking. I
look over at Arba, and see her long, dark hair
spread out on the pillow, and her favorite
teddy bear sleeping next to her.

As I walk into the bedroom that I share with
Monie and Chantelle, I see Monie sitting at my
computer. Why did she have to come home

tonight? I want to tell her to go talk on the phone or something, like she always does. I need to check my e-mail, and see if any of the Cheetah Girls are in the Phat Planet chat room.

Why is she always hogging *my* computer? When our super, Mr. Hammer, gave me the computer, Mrs. Bosco said that I should share it with Monie and Chantelle. Well, I don't want to!

"Are you gonna be a long time?" I ask, hoping Monie doesn't give me a hard time.

"Nah, I just gotta finish this letter for my nurse's aide application," she says, taking her bubble gum out of her mouth and twirling it around her finger, then putting it back in.

"Everybody in the building's heard about Gaye, so I thought I'd better come home and help Mrs. Bosco if she needed it," Monie says without turning her head. "I saw the thing on the news about her, too."

"Yeah, I heard about it—she was really on the news?" I ask, curious.

"No, Dorinda, *she* wasn't on the news—they were just talking about her. They showed her picture, and left a number if anybody had information, that type of thing," Monie says, getting an attitude.

"Oh. That's what Ms. Keisha said."

"What would Ms. Keisha know? She can't even get a job."

I guess now that Monie is applying for a nurse's aide position, she thinks someone is gonna hire her with that nasty attitude? If you ask me, she might as well head down to the unemployment line, and fill out an application early, you know what I'm saying?

"You gonna get a job?" I ask, curious to see what she's gonna say. I can't imagine her being anybody's nurse's aide. She didn't even know what to do when Mrs. Bosco got a bronchitis attack last winter. *I* was the one to call for an ambulance to take her to the hospital. Monie just stood around, acting all scared. *I'd* be scared to see Monie with a thermometer, trying to take someone's temperature—she'd probably stick the patient in the eye with it or something!

"I don't know, Dorinda, but I'm sure gonna do something to get outta here, that's all I know," she snorts at me. "There. I'm finished. Go on and use the computer."

I feel angry that she doesn't say *your* computer, but I don't say anything, because I don't want to get into a fight with her. I decide to go into the Phat Planet chat room first, because somebody from my crew is probably there. Knowing Chanel, she probably needs someone to talk to, sitting up there in bed with her ankle elevated on a pillow, or getting treated to an ice pack on her butt!

The first person I see, typing madly in the chat room, is supa-tasty "LimpCutie." I should have known Tiffany wouldn't have wasted any time hogging up the chat room! Why did I even tell her about it? Of course, Tiffany recognizes my log-on name, "Uptown Hoodie"—and I can almost hear her squealing with delight, just by her greeting.

UPTOWN HOODIE—IT'S ME, HANGING WITH THE POSSE!

HI, LIMPCUTIE, I type back, so I don't bust her cover, but I really would like to tell her to "scram and take the Spam"—or something that Galleria would riff when she gets mad.

I GOTTA TELL YOU SOMETHING, she types on the screen. GUESS WHO WAS ON TELEVISION TONIGHT, TALKING ABOUT FOSTER CHILDREN?

I KNOW—MARIAH CAREY, I type back.

YES, MAMACITA—MAYBE WE CAN GET TO MEET HER?

I can't believe it, but Tiffany is always

angling for *something*. She's worse than Galleria! What does she think—just because Mariah Carey does a public service announcement for foster children, we're gonna get to meet her? I wanna scream at my clueless sister, "Get a grip, Tiff!"

All of a sudden, I notice that Galleria is online. WAZZUP, UPTOWN HOODIE? she types. I SEE YOU HANGING WITH SOME NEW CREW, RIGHT?

IT'S MY SISTER, I type back.

YOU'RE JOKING OR SMOKING? Galleria types on the screen.

NO, I'M NOT.

SEEMS LIKE THE TWO OF YOU ARE HANGING TIGHT LATELY, DON'T YOU THINK? Galleria types—and knowing her, there is more to that nibble than a piece of cheese.

NOT EXACTLY, I explain, then realize that Tiffany is "seeing" everything I say, so I'd better mention that she wants to audition for the Cheetah Girls. LISTEN, WHAT TIFFANY WANTS TO KNOW IS, CAN SHE SING FOR US?

SOMEONE MUST'VE CHANGED THE CHANNEL TO A TELEMONDO STATION! types Chanel, who is also in the chat room. Galleria must've beeped her. I know they have a secret code when they want to talk online. I'm gonna get a beeper soon, too.

SHE WANTS TO TRY OUT FOR THE GROUP, THAT'S ALL I'M TALKING ABOUT.

WHY DIDN'T YOU TELL US BEFORE? Galleria challenges me.

I KNOW, BUT WITH EVERYTHING GOING ON, I THOUGHT I SHOULD ASK NOW.

HI, GALLERIA! LimpCutie types, breaking into the conversation.

YOU WANNA RIFF WITH US SOMETIME? Galleria asks Tiffany.

YES!

CHANEL NO. 5, YOU WANNA HAVE SOME COMPANY TOMORROW NIGHT? Galleria asks, using Chuchie's onscreen name.

ESTÁ BIEN WITH ME!

When I sign off to Tiffany, I can't help but crack a joke. SEE YOU TOMORROW NITE AT CHANEL'S CRIB, LIMPCUTIE—BUT DON'T EXPECT MARIAH CAREY TO BE IN THE HOUSE CHECKING OUT YOUR AUDITION!

HEY, UPTOWN HOODIE, YOU NEVER KNOW! IF MAMACITA MARIAH KNEW HOW DOPE I WUZ, SHE WOULD FLUTTER HER WINGS LIKE A BUTTERFLY JUST TO SEE ME! SO WHY DON'T YOU CALL HER AND INVITE HER?

What was I thinking, inviting Tiffany to sing for the Cheetah Girls? Well, I didn't exactly invite her—Galleria did. I think Bubbles's invitation was more like a challenge to her, though.

My biology teacher, Mr. Roundworm, says genes have a mind of their own, and they do exactly as they please. Maybe he's right, 'cuz my sister Tiffany is definitely popping kernels in her own microwave, if you know what I'm saying!

Chapter 8

I haven't said anything about the Kats and Kittys drama to my crew, and I hope none of them bring it up. Mrs. Bosco is right—I shouldn't look any gift horse in the mouth, just check to make sure it has hooves. I know that my crew is down with me, so I shouldn't sweat it.

Oh, now I get it—maybe that's what Mrs. Bosco meant about the hooves part. Just make sure your friends—or the "gift horse"—are for *real*. Yeah, well my crew still blabbed their big mouths—and told *everybody* in the Kats and Kittys Klub that I'm a foster child—like *my* face should be on a poster, begging for donations or something!

Well, now I'm about to be face-to-face with my crew. They arrived at Chanel's house before I did, since I had to work my three-hour shift at the YMCA, then come back downtown to SoHo, where Chanel lives. Believe me, I was real glad to get some duckets in my pocket, though.

Aqua beams when she sees me—which makes me feel good to see my crew. That is, until Galleria asks, "What did Mrs. Bosco say about the donation?"

"You know, she thought it was cool," I say, but I can hear how choked my voice sounds.

"Dorinda . . . I, um, we thought it was okay to tell everybody about your situation," Aqua says earnestly. "It was Indigo's idea to put ACS on the charity voting ballot, because she saw Gaye on the news, too."

No wonder Indigo was so nice to me! The whole world saw Gaye on the news but me! Now my crew is standing around the living room, looking at me like I'm a lost puppy who needs a bone—and a home.

"I just wish you didn't tell *everybody*!" I blurt out, tears springing to my eyes.

"We're real sorry," Angie pipes up.

"Okay, squash it," I say, when I hear Pucci's footsteps running down the hallway.

"*Mami* made stuff for your friends," Pucci says to Chanel. His eyes twinkling, he motions for us to come into the dining room.

Chanel hobbles in first. The table is covered with a pretty pink flowered tablecloth, and matching paper cups, napkins, and plates. From the looks of the food on the table, I can tell Chanel is definitely milking her sprained ankle for points. She even got Mrs. Simmons to make *plántanos* (fried plantains) and Dominican-style *pollo caliente* (spicy chicken wings and drumsticks) for us to snack on.

Now, looking at the food, I realize how hungry I am. I'm not sure if you're supposed to eat these things with your fingers or a knife and fork, so I wait until I see Galleria take one of the legs, put it daintily on her paper napkin, then eat it with her fingers. I do exactly as she does, including lifting my pinkie finger higher for effect.

Galleria, Chanel, Aqua, and Angie decide to sit down at the dining room table, while we wait for Tiffany to get here. After we get our grub on, the plan is that we are gonna hang out in Mrs. Simmons's big exercise studio, and sing a little with Tiffany. Pucci has already put a folding chair in the studio so Chanel can sit down. Even though her tailbone is healed, Chanel still has to stay off her badly sprained ankle as much as possible.

I think Chanel feels kinda lonely that we didn't come over and rehearse at her house last week. Pucci is being nice to Chanel too, which I can't believe! "Chanel, you want something to drink?" he asks.

"A Dominican cocktail, *por favor!*" Chanel says, milking Pucci for more points. Even though the pitcher of Mrs. Simmons's Dominican cocktail (I think it's mango and cranberry juice with tropical punch) is right in the middle of the table, Pucci pours it for Chanel.

Mrs. Simmons turns on the radio, then places some pretty crystal glasses back in the breakfront. Wow, all the crystal sparkling in the breakfront makes the room look really fancy!

"You girls have fun, but I've got to get back to work, because I'm on deadline," Mrs. Simmons says. But she keeps lingering in the dining room, doing things.

The radio deejay announces the Mariah Carey concert on Friday night.

"I wish they were giving away some free tickets, shoot," Angie blurts out.

"I wish we could just pay and go!" Chanel pipes up, loud enough for her mother to hear.

"Chanel, how are you going to go to a concert on crutches? *Dígame!*" Mrs. Simmons snaps. "Tell me that—even if you had the money?"

"What happened?" Chanel counters, getting that innocent look on her face, like she doesn't know what she said. "Disabled people get to go places too, *Mamí!*"

"I know, Chanel," Mrs. Simmons shoots back, like she's embarrassed. I wonder why Mrs. Simmons keeps lingering in the dining room area, even though she says she has work to do on that book she's writing. I think she wants to see what my sister Tiffany looks like or something, because she turns and asks me, "Where does your sister go to school?"

I freeze for a second, because I can't remember. Then it pops back into my head. "Um, St. Agnes of the Peril."

"Oh, private Catholic school," Mrs. Simmons says, like she's impressed.

"Uh-huh."

Pushing up the sleeves on her pretty pink

furry cardigan sweater, Mrs. Simmons keeps at it. "So how much younger is she than you?"

I almost choke on my chicken wing! Why is Mrs. Simmons being so nosy? Even Galleria pauses her chomp and looks up at me!

"Um, a year," I say, my stomach starting to get a bad case of the squigglies. Inside, I'm shrieking, *Please don't ask me any more questions about Tiffany!*

"So . . . she's thirteen?" Mrs. Simmons continues absentmindedly, now arranging some silver knives in the breakfront drawer.

For a split second, I wonder if I should tell a fib-eroni. Then I realize that eventually my crew is gonna find out that I'm only twelve years old, and not fourteen like they are—even though I'm in the ninth grade, too. "No, um, she's eleven," I say. Then I wait for the sky to fall on my head like Chicken Little.

Everybody stops and looks at me. I guess Chanel is better at math than she thinks, because she's the first one to say, "What happened? Do' Re Mi, how old are you?"

"T-twelve," I say, fighting back the tears.

"How could you be twelve years old!?" Aqua asks, so shocked that her eyes are bugging out.

The twins are still thirteen, see. Their grand-mother sent them to school early, because she thought they were so smart. Well, now my crew knows how smart *I* am—or how *stupid*, for try-ing to tell a fib-eroni on the sneak tip!

"I got skipped twice already," I say apologetically.

"That's nothing to be ashamed of, Dorinda," Mrs. Simmons says, surprised.

"I'm sorry I didn't tell you before," I say, looking straight at Galleria, then Chanel, then Aqua and Angie. "I was embarrassed."

"You *should* be sorry for telling us a fib-eroni," Galleria snorts. "We tell you *everything*."

"Well, you didn't tell me you were going to blab to everybody in the whole world that I live in a foster home!" I blurt out. Just then, the doorbell rings. Galleria and I lock stares for a sec, before we're distracted by loud giggling coming from the hallway.

"*Mami*, she has a Flammerstein Schwimmer scooter like I do!" Pucci says excitedly, riding his fancy-schmancy scooter into the dining area. It looks just like the one I saw in Tiffany's bedroom, except the knobs on Pucci's are acid green, and Tiffany's are neon pink.

"Pucci—don't make me take that thing away from you!" Mrs. Simmons yells. Then she notices Tiffany, and smiles a big, phony smile.

I feel so embarrassed when I see how corny Tiffany's outfit is. Now she's wearing a cheetah knit cap with a pom-pom on top, a matching cheetah sweat jacket, and a white skort—you know, the kind with shorts underneath. I notice how red her thighs are—probably because they're freezing to death. I look down at her feet to see why she looks so tall. I can't believe it—she went and got black Madd Monster shoes, just like mine!

"Aren't your legs cold?" Mrs. Simmons asks Tiffany, causing *everybody* to notice how short her skirt is, and making me more embarrassed than I already am!

"No," Tiffany says, giggling nervously.

"You have a funny giggle!" Pucci blurts out.

"I do," Tiffany says, giggling even more!

Chanel says something in Spanish to Pucci, which I don't understand, and he runs out of the dining room area.

"I like your shoes," Chanel coos to Tiffany.

"Thanks," she says, and now she's blushing. "I got the same ones Dorinda has."

"Come get your grub on," Galleria says, chuckling to Tiffany.

"Oh, thanks," she says, licking her lips.

"Of course. It ain't no thing but a chicken wing!" Galleria riffs, handing her a paper plate.

"You're the one who rhymes all the time, right?" Tiffany asks Galleria, like she's a famous singer or something.

Galleria giggles, but at least she doesn't snarkle the way Tiffany does. I'm trying to check out Galleria, Chanel, and the twins on the sneak tip, to see how they're feeling Tiffany. I can't believe Galleria hasn't said anything about Tiffany's outfit! Galleria's motto is, "You definitely don't wear white after Labor Day, or before Memorial Day." But Galleria is definitely on her best behavior tonight.

After we finish our munch, my crew starts "chatting" with Tiffany. Please don't let them ask her anything about this adoption situation, or our mother!

But I can tell that Galleria is angling for some info about our situation. And just like I thought would happen, Galleria asks Tiffany how she found out she was adopted!

"I found the key to my parents' safe-deposit

box!" Tiffany squeals with delight. "It took me two Saturday afternoons."

"You work fast, girlina," Galleria squeals back. "I'll make sure to keep you away from the jewel vault when I get one!"

I should have known those two would hit it off. Tiffany tells Bubbles every last detail, and Galleria just pries it out of her, like clues to an unsolved mystery.

"Dorinda, you know I've been hearing melodies all day to that song I wrote about you—'Do' Re Mi on the Q.T.'"

Why would Galleria bring that song up now? That's the one she wrote when she found out Tiffany was my sister. See, at first, I didn't tell my crew about Tiffany coming to find me. But when she showed up at the Apollo Theatre with her parents, to watch us compete in the Battle of the Divettes, I was busted—cold!

Afterward, Galleria wrote a song about it, because she said I'm the most secretive person she's ever met. Now she wants to sing the song in front of Tiffany! Where's the Sandman from the Apollo when you need him to drag her away, huh?

"Tiffany, why don't we all sing the song

together?" Galleria says, popping a track into the cassette.

"This is a master jammy whammy," Galleria explains. "See, Ms. Dorothea gets these phat club tapes made by some deejay, and we use them for rehearsing and performing."

"I know what this song is!" Tiffany says, excited. "It's from Mariah Carey's *Rainbow* album."

"Yeah, you're right," Aqua says, then looks at Tiffany. "Dorinda said you've got a real nice keyboard. How'd you learn to play?"

"I taught myself," Tiffany says proudly.

"You didn't know how to play the piano or anything?" Aqua asks, impressed. The twins go to LaGuardia Performing Arts High School, and even though they don't play any instruments, there are a lot of music majors in the mix at their school.

"No," Tiffany says proudly. "I didn't."

"Well, we've gotta come over sometime, and see your magic keyboard!" Angie jokes.

Tiffany takes her seriously, and says, "When do you wanna come?"

"Girlinas, we have to get back to the beat," Galleria cuts in. We all go stand next to Chanel, so she doesn't have to move her chair, and get ready to harmonize. This is what I love most about being in a singing group—just riffing together in rehearsal. When you're onstage, it's a lot more scary.

"Okay, let's sing the part, right after the lead, in C minor, and the chorus in B flat."

"Okay!" Tiffany says excitedly.

Galleria hands us each a copy of the song, then starts the intro. Chanel joins in, and then we're all supposed to sing the rest of the lead together:

"This is Galleria
and this is Chanel
coming to you live
From Cheetah Girls Central.
Where we process data that matters
And even mad chatter
But today we're here to tell you
About our friend, Do' Re Mi
(That's Miss Dorinda to you)
Kats and Kittys, the drama
Has gotten so radikkio
Just when we thought we knew our crew
Bam! The scandal was told!"

Finally, Galleria makes the motion for us to stop singing.

I know exactly why, too. Tiffany sings like a daffy dolphin—you know, Flipper, under water! Galleria looks at her and says, "Tiffany, sing the lead by yourself."

Tiffany gets all shy, and says, "I don't want to."

"Come on, Tiffany, we're just flowing!" Galleria says, prodding her along.

"Okay," Tiffany finally agrees, then giggles some more. "'But today we're here to tell you/About our friend, Do' Re Mi/That's Miss Dorinda to you!'" Tiffany sings, but then stops.

I take back what I said earlier—Tiffany sings *worse* than Flipper.

"Tiffany—you're um, gonna need a lot of vocal training to be able to sing with us," Galleria says slowly.

All of a sudden, I feel protective toward Tiffany. Please don't let Galleria go off on my sister!

"Um, yeah, I know," Tiffany says, smiling in that innocent way that she does. "But maybe I could play the keyboard in the group?"

Tiffany just won't quit.

"Tiffany, the Cheetah Girls are all singers," Galleria says. "I mean, Chanel, Dorinda, and I don't sing as well as Aqua and Angie do, but we've still had a lot of training." I can't believe how nice she's being to Tiffany! "I mean, we could play the keyboard together sometimes, for fun and stuff. That would be cool, right?" Galleria looks around at all of us for approval.

"Yeah, maybe that would help our rehearsals and stuff," I say, sticking up for Tiffany.

"Yeah," Chanel pipes up. "I wanna learn it, too!"

"But I wanna be *in* the Cheetah Girls," Tiffany says, pouting.

"Well, let's just wait and see," Galleria says finally.

Tiffany beams, like she's accepting an award or something. Then she lets out that hyena snarkle that makes everybody giggle, and we goof around for a while before Mrs. Simmons comes inside the studio and tells us it's time to go home.

We all burst into another round of giggles before we wiggle our separate ways home. Thank God for my crew—and Tiffany, too. I can't believe they found such a dope way out of this sticky situation! Letting Tiffany hang and play keyboard with us at rehearsals without letting her be in the group is a stroke of genius!

Chapter 9

I sneak into my apartment like a mouse on the nibble tip, because it's *really* late, and I don't want to wake my foster mother or my brothers and sisters, who are usually snoozing by this time. Mr. Bosco has probably already left. He usually stops by the Lenox Café before he heads up to the Bronx to his job and begins his graveyard shift at the stroke of midnight.

My heart starts pounding when I open the door—and see Mrs. Bosco and most of my foster brothers and sisters, all sitting in the living room! They're obviously waiting for me—everybody except for Arba, who is probably sleeping.

"What are y'all doing up?" I ask, trying to act

supa cool, even though my voice is squeaking even more than the front door.

Something must be wrong. I look over at Gaye, to see if I can peep this situation, but she is sitting quietly on the couch next to Mrs. Bosco, sucking her thumb. Maybe they found Gaye's mother, and she's gonna be leaving us pretty soon or something.

Twinkie runs over to me and gives me a supa-dupa hug. "We're gonna see the Butterfly lady tomorrow!" she squeals.

"Really?" I say, humoring Twinkie. Next she'll be telling me that Dorothy from *The Wizard of Oz* called and invited us to a picnic over the rainbow, you know what I'm saying?

"We're *all* going to see her!" Twinkie adds adamantly.

"Now, Rita, why you telling Dorinda that?" Mrs. Bosco says. Then she stops abruptly, because she's gonna break into one of her coughing spells. Her bronchitis is acting up again, now that it's getting cold outside. "I told you, we're gonna let Dorinda de—"

Finally, a cough catches up with Mrs. Bosco and she starts hacking. Then she tries to finish her sentence before it subsides—"decide how we gonna split up the t-t-t-t-ickets."

Did I hear her right?

Mrs. Bosco reaches over to the end table—but Nestor yells, "I got it, Mrs. Bosco!" He hops off the living room floor where he was perched, grabs the newspaper off the end table, and hands it to her with a big smile. *He* seems really excited, too, just like Twinkie.

Mrs. Bosco rests the newspaper on her lap, then takes out her wrinkled handkerchief—the one she always keeps in her dress pocket. I feel stupid standing there in the middle of the living room floor—like I've been called down to detention or something in school. I just can't wait until someone tells me what's going on! Finally, Mrs. Bosco opens up the newspaper, and points to a photo that I can't make out from where I'm standing.

"Go ahead and read it yourself, Dorinda," Mrs. Bosco says, handing me the newspaper. "It's too dark in here for me to read it to you, even with my glasses on."

"Okay." I move closer, and take the newspaper from her hand. This is one of the games we play—see, I know she's illiterate, even though I pretend I don't.

I stand next to the lamp by the end table and look at the photo Mrs. Bosco pointed to. It's a head shot of Mariah Carey, just sorta smiling. Then I read the small caption below her picture: "'Pop star Mariah Carey, a longtime spokesperson for New York City foster children, was so moved by the Eyewitness News report on the abandoned child found in Coney Island, that she has provided tickets to her Madison Square Concert tomorrow night for the foster family that took in the toddler. Ms. Carey could not be reached at press time, but her spokesperson says the Administration of Children's Services will be handling arrangements for the family to attend the sold-out concert.'"

"Are they talking about *us*?" I ask in disbelief.

"I guess so," Mrs. Bosco says with a satisfied smile, shifting her weight on the couch. Gaye peers up at me quickly with her intense black eyes, then quickly hides her face behind Mrs. Bosco's ample arm.

"Ms. Keisha saw the paper first—and by the time she came into the laundry room and told me, she'd already told everybody in the building about it. She wouldn't even let me keep her paper!" Mrs. Bosco says, shaking her head.

I can feel my cheeks burning. How come nobody told me about the article in the newspaper?

"Of course, Skip didn't have any more news-papers left," Mrs. Bosco says, rubbing her legs. "'Cuz those knuckleheads on the corner done stole half of them from him at the crack of dawn. So I had to go all the way over to the Korean place on Malcolm X Boulevard and buy one. You'd think Ms. Keisha coulda bothered to tell me that before I went all the way over to Skip's, but she's too busy acting like she *is* the newspaper!"

"How—?" I start to ask, but Mrs. Bosco is just getting started.

"Of course, Manty Clarke was over there buy-ing a Lotto ticket, and he had the nerve to invite *himself* to the concert," Mrs. Bosco says, sound-ing pleased with herself. "I told that toothless fool he'd have more luck striking a deal with the tooth fairy to get tickets—and he just might get some new front teeth in the bargain!"

Khalil cracks up at Mrs. Bosco's joke, which snaps me out of my daze. I don't know why I'm upset, anyway. It figures that nosy Ms. Keisha—and everybody in the building—already knew about this before I found out.

Nobody cares enough to tell me anything first.

"And then Mrs. Tattle called here after you had already left for school," Mrs. Bosco says, yawning. She's probably been telling this story all day. "She sounded real pleased with herself, that's for sure. She said everybody down at the agency was real excited. I figured they would be—anything that gets their names in the papers when they ain't been accused of doing something wrong, like they always do."

"I wish somebody had told me before now," I say, disappointed that I wasn't here when the whole thing jumped off.

"Ain't you glad we're going to see Mariah Carey?" Khalil blurts out, making me feel embarrassed again.

"Of course I am," I say, trying to sound more excited about the whole situation. "What did Mrs. Tattle say when she called?"

"Just what it says there in the newspaper," Mrs. Bosco says, scratching her wig. "What's that you call her, Rita?"

"The Butterfly lady!" Twinkie says proudly, twirling herself on the couch.

"That's right—she said that the Butterfly lady gave us some tickets to go to her concert—

free tickets—otherwise I woulda told Mrs. Tattle she could keep them, 'cuz Mariah ain't paying no bills around here," Mrs. Bosco says, nodding her head.

I guess Mrs. Bosco sees the confused look on my face, because she adds, "I told her I was gonna put you in charge of the situation, 'cause you're the musical one around here. So I said to leave those tickets in an envelope at the box office with your name on it. Don't worry, ain't nobody can touch those tickets but you. I figured you'd wanna invite your friends."

"Oh, okay!" I say, my face lighting up. This is gonna be so dope—*me*, finally doing something for my crew! Now I feel stupid for getting upset. I guess Mrs. Bosco couldn't call me at school, because I don't have a cell phone or beeper, like Galleria and Chanel have. I wish I did have one—then I would know about things right when they're jumping off, like they do. But I'm just so excited—for the first time in my life, I've got something nobody else has! Finally, I get to be the lucky one!

"You know, it would be nice if you invited your sister, too," Mrs. Bosco says. She turns to Chantelle, who is sitting by the edge of the end table, fiddling with something. "Stop playing with the coasters—they're already raggedy enough as it is."

I wonder which sister she's talking about. I don't want to be sitting at a Mariah Carey concert with Monie the Meanie, acting like she's not having a good time, the way she always does. She thinks everything is corny—including me being in the Cheetah Girls.

"Um, you mean Monie?" I ask, waiting for the response.

"No, Dorinda. I mean that child Tiffany," Mrs. Bosco says, peering at me over her bifocals as if she's wondering why I'm being so dim-witty or something.

Why should I invite Tiffany? Mrs. Bosco must realize that I've gotta invite my whole crew before I invite anyone else. It's not like Mariah Carey's peeps have given us a dozen tickets or something like that, you know what I'm saying?

"But I should invite Twinkie—um, Rita, and—" I start in, getting defensive.

"I wanna go!" Nestor blurts out, cutting me off.

"I wanna go, too," says Khalil, sulking.

"How you divide the twenty-five tickets,

Dorinda, is your business," Mrs. Bosco says matter-of-factly.

"Did you say *twenty-five* tickets?" I ask, dumbfounded.

"That's what I been trying to tell you this whole time. Mrs. Tattle says they left twenty-five tickets for you at the box office," Mrs. Bosco says, like I should get with the program.

"That's so dope!" I say, finally getting excited. I plop down my backpack and take out my notebook and a pencil, so I can make a list of everyone I'm going to invite. "O-kay," I say out loud, flipping to an empty page.

Nestor, Khalil, and Kenya are pushing at each other, trying to get a look, but then I stop and look down at Mrs. Bosco. "Are you *sure* they said *twenty-five* tickets?"

"Dorinda, if you ask me again, I'm gonna tell Mrs. Tattle to give those tickets to somebody else, 'cuz you don't want 'em," Mrs. Bosco says, chuckling. "As a matter of fact, I'm gonna tell her to give them to Ms. Keisha!"

"Awright!" I say, jumping up and down. Twinkie grabs my waist and jumps up and down, too. "Okay!" I say again, looking around at all my foster brothers and sisters. "Who wants to go see Mariah Carey?"

"Me!" screams Twinkie.

At the top of the list, I write: Twinkie. Galleria. Chanel. Aqua. Angie. Tiffany. Me. That makes seven. I can't believe I still have eighteen tickets left! "Do *you* wanna go?" I ask Mrs. Bosco, embarrassed because I didn't even think of asking her first.

"Oh, no, that's for you younguns'—first fool that stepped on my foot, or pushed into me, and I'd be outta there," Mrs. Bosco says.

"But you're the one they gave the tickets to," I protest. If it wasn't for Mrs. Bosco taking in Gaye, we wouldn't be getting to go see Mariah Carey, you know what I'm saying? Suddenly I feel bad. I'll bet Mrs. Bosco doesn't want to come because she's not feeling well.

"No, Dorinda. I'm not going to be sitting up there with all those screaming fools. Now you know I can't let you go without an adult chaperone, so I figured you'd invite Galleria's mother. She is you girls' manager, after all," Mrs. Bosco says proudly. For the first time, I realize Mrs. Bosco really is proud that I'm in a singing group.

"You sure you don't want to go?" I ask her

again, ignoring Khalil, Nestor, and now Kenya's whining.

"Dorinda," Mrs. Bosco starts in, but I already know what she's gonna say, so I cut her off before she finishes.

"I know, if I ask you one more time," I say, finishing her sentence.

"That's right."

"Okay. Ms. Dorothea and Mr. Garibaldi will be our chaperones, and maybe Ms. Simmons, too." I write down their names, and then I think maybe I should invite Pucci, too. I'll ask Chanel. She may not want her mom hanging out with us, 'cuz now that she's been cooped up in the house with a sprained ankle, Chanel wants to get away from her.

This whole thing is so dope, I can't believe it's happening! Wait till I get online and talk to my crew! I feel so excited that I look over at Gaye and smile, even though I think she is probably scared of me. I wonder if I should bring her, too? Maybe not. What if she throws a fit in public? She would probably be frightened by all those people anyway.

As if reading my mind, Mrs. Bosco says, "I don't think it would be a good idea to bring

Gaye. You go on and have a good time."

"Okay," I say, writing down Pucci's name next.

"I wanna come!" Twinkie says for the fiftieth time.

"Rita, you're going—now go on to bed," Mrs. Bosco says, yawning. "I let you stay up so we could tell Dorinda, but it's time for *all of y'all* to go to bed."

Twinkie kisses me good night, and Mrs. Bosco takes Gaye by the arm to bring her into her bedroom. I say good-bye to Gaye, but she doesn't answer. I feel so bad for her. I know how mad she's gonna be when she's old enough to figure out what happened to her. Just like I was.

After Pucci's name, I write: Khalil. Nestor. Shawn. Okay, that makes fourteen people so far. I might invite Kenya—even though she's only six, and this is a concert for grown-ups. Topwe, Arba, and Corky are also pretty young.

Even though it kills me, I write down Chantelle and Monie. I know Monie's gonna want to bring her boyfriend—but that's too bad, 'cuz I can't invite everybody. Maybe I should go see if she's here.

Before I even walk into the bedroom, Monie,

who is propped on her bed like she's been waiting for me, blurts out, "I'm not going if you don't invite Hector, too."

"Okay," I say, giving in right away, because I don't want to fight with her. I don't want to be with her at the concert anyway, and if Hector is with her, she won't be on my case, you know what I'm saying?

Monie throws me a fake smile, then decides to pick a fight with me anyway. "I don't understand why Mrs. Bosco put *you* in charge of the tickets. *I'm* the oldest—she shoulda given them to *me*."

I can't believe Monie is trying to start a beef jerky about *that*. Where is she when Mrs. Bosco needs to pay bills, write letters to her sisters and brothers in North Carolina, or has to fill out reports for the foster care agency, huh? Mrs. Bosco doesn't ask Monie to write stuff for her— she asks *me*.

But right now, I don't have time to deal with Monie the Meanie, who is definitely earning her nickname to the max. All I can think of right now is getting online and talking with my crew.

"I didn't ask to be in charge of the tickets, okay?" I turn and say without thinking.

"Yeah, well, as long as you give me two, I don't care," Monie says. Propping herself up on her elbows, she adds, "I want you to give me the tickets, too, 'cuz I don't want to go with y'all. I'm gonna be over at Hector's house—and I'll leave from there."

"Um, that's cool with me, except the tickets are at the box office with my name on them," I reply matter-of-factly. That should squash this situation for real. Like it or not, the least Monie can do is come with us as a family.

"Awright, but don't expect me to be hanging with y'all," Monie says, sucking her teeth. Then she reaches under her pillow and puts on her Walkman headphones. I wonder where she got that from?

Probably Hector bought it for her. He's seventeen, and works full-time at Radio Shack 'cuz he dropped out of school. Monie told us about it like it was something to brag about, you know what I'm saying? No way would I drop out of high school. I'm gonna go to college, too—even if the Cheetah Girls blow up.

"That's cool with me," I say, trying to be chill. I open up the third drawer in the bureau, which is my drawer, and pull out my checkered pajamas. "Just meet us outside of Madison Square Garden at six-thirty."

"Six-thirty?" Monie says, getting an attitude. "Why so early?"

"'Cuz you never know if there's gonna be a long line or something," I say, feeling stupid. Maybe it is too early to go there, but I don't want to mess this up. "It is a Mariah Carey concert, Monie."

Monie acts like she doesn't hear me, but that's okay. If she isn't there at six-thirty, then we're gonna go inside without her. The heck with it, I decide. Mariah Carey invited the *family* that took in Gaye, so that means we're *all* going. I open my notebook again, and write down some more names: Hector. 17. Kenya. 18. Topwe. 19. Corky. 20. Arba. 21. Looking at all the names on the list again, I feel satisfied, so I close my notebook and put in on my nightstand.

I try to listen if Mrs. Bosco is still up, but I don't hear anything, so I tiptoe into the living room again. I don't think she'll mind if I use the telephone to call Galleria and Chanel. I have to beep them—putting 911 after their phone number, so they'll know to answer the page 'cuz it's important. Then they'll contact the twins.

I realize that maybe I should wait till tomorrow. But as I get near the telephone, and see that the coast is clear, I decide to call them anyway. Why should I wait? No way, José! My crew is gonna want the lowdown to this showdown—even if the crows are crowing, and the roosters are up singing cock-a-doodle-doo!

Chapter 10

I was so glad when school was over today, because Galleria and Chanel went
around telling *everybody*—even Teqwuila and
Kadeesha, whom they *never* talk to unless it's to
squash a beef jerky—that I got twenty-five free
tickets to the Mariah Carey concert tonight!
Fashion Industries peeps were having Gucci
Envy attacks all over the place!

Then I started feeling bad, because I couldn't
invite everybody I'm cool with at school. In the
end, I did invite LaRonda Jones from math
class on the sneak tip. I *had* to hook her up,
because she hooked me up once.

See, when we made our Cheetah Girls chok-
ers, we sold them to peeps at school—but they

ended up falling apart before first period was over—and LaRonda was the only one who was cool about the situation. I made LaRonda *promise* that she wouldn't go around telling everybody I invited her to Mariah's concert.

I'm sorry, but I can't help it if I'm a little superstitious. What if I drag all these people to Madison Square Garden, and there is no envelope with my name on it, huh? All I'm saying is, it wouldn't be the first time Mrs. Bosco got things mixed up. I'll never forget how embarrassed I was when I had to finally tell my crew that my adoption didn't go through, because Mrs. Bosco didn't understand the paperwork and the whole adoption procedure.

Just after I finish getting dressed up for the concert, someone knocks on my open bedroom door, and I turn to see who it is.

"How do I *loook*, Dorinda?" Topwe asks me in his funny African accent. He grins, showing off that big gap in his front teeth that always always makes me smile. Topwe then strikes a pose in the doorway, fingering the burgundy bow tie he's wearing with his white shirt and gray pants.

"You look dope!" I say, noticing that the sores

by his mouth look like crusty critters. Topwe's HIV virus has been acting up lately, and he even had to stay home from school all week. But he's been feeling better since yesterday, and anyhow, nothing was gonna keep him from going to the Mariah Carey concert. Not even HIV!

"Come here, lemme put a little lotion on that handsome face." I grab the bottle of Magik Potion lotion, and rub some all over Topwe's face. I don't think the stuff is magic as much as it's just plain greasy.

I'm so glad I decided to invite all my brothers and sisters to the concert, even if they don't know who Mariah Carey is. I can tell they are just happy to be going somewhere, because we never really do stuff together like a real family, you know what I'm saying?

I put on my cheetah bell-bottoms and matching jacket, then look at myself in the mirror on the back of the closet door. Today, *I'm* the cheetah who's got something to growl about! Taking another long look, I decide that I need a few sparkles around my eyes, then I'm good to go. I open a pot of Manic Panic gold glitter and dab it on.

Twinkie runs into my bedroom without

knocking first, but I don't say anything, even though she knows she's not supposed to do that. "Can I have some?" she asks, eyeing my glitter. She reaches for the jar, dropping a candy wrapper on the floor.

"Go ahead," I tell her, but I dab on the gel for her. Twinkie turns to run out of my bedroom, but I yell after her, "Pick up the wrapper you dropped. You know Cheetah Girls don't litter, they glitter!"

"Yes, Cheetah Bunny," Twinkie squeals, throwing the wrapper into my garbage can and running out again. "I'll go get everybody."

When I come out of my bedroom, I'm surprised that Mrs. Bosco is wearing her nice brown corduroy jumper and her "good wig."

"I guess I might as well see what all this ruckus is about," she says, still brushing her wig into place.

"Of course," I chuckle. Now I realize that I was right. She *wasn't* feeling well yesterday. As if she's reading my mind, Mrs. Bosco goes on to say, "I must say I'm feeling pretty good today."

"You look good, too," I chuckle, helping her on with her jacket.

Now I'm wondering what we're gonna do

about Gaye. "Is Gaye, um, coming with us?"

"Yes, indeed—unless you done gave away all the tickets," Mrs. Bosco asks.

"No," I say, feeling embarrassed. I'm not going to tell her that I didn't invite twenty-five people because I felt kinda scared about this whole thing not coming off.

"I think Gaye will be fine. I'll just stay close to her," Mrs. Bosco explains, like she's trying to reassure me or something. Then she goes into the kitchen.

Gaye is sitting quietly on the couch, waiting. She is wearing one of Arba's pink jumpers, and a pretty pink bow in her braid on top.

"You look pretty, Gaye," I say, but I don't expect her to answer me, so I just turn to go back in my bedroom and get my backpack.

"*Tank* you," she says quietly.

At first, I'm startled that Gaye has actually said something to me, but I try not to make a big deal out of it. I smile at her again, but she quickly puts her head down. Walking into my bedroom, I realize that Ms. Keisha is right as usual—Gaye *does* have a West Indian accent.

"Monie's gonna meet us at the Garden, so we should all go downstairs to wait for Mr.

Garibaldi," I yell to Mrs. Bosco from the front door. I get everyone out the door, and we're off to the concert!

I'm so glad that Ms. Dorothea and Mr. Garibaldi are coming. Mr. Garibaldi, or Franco, as he insists I call him, even volunteered to pick up my family and drive us down to Madison Square Garden, since he has a big van that he uses to bring clothes from his factory in Brooklyn to their boutique in SoHo.

Mr. Walker, the twins' father, is gonna pick up Ms. Dorothea, Galleria, and Chanel and bring them to the Garden with the twins. Mr. Walker has a Bronco, and sometimes he and Mr. Garibaldi try to outdo each other over who's driving who, if you know what I'm saying.

While we stand outside our building, waiting for Mr. Garibaldi, some of our neighbors give us a shout-out. You'd think we won the lottery or something!

"I can't believe y'all are going to see Miss Mariah. I wish I was going. Don't forget to bring me back a CD, or a T-shirt, or *something*," yells Ms. Keisha, sticking her head out the window, her bright pink hair rollers bobbing all over the place as she laughs.

"Well, you'd better settle for an empty pop-corn container, 'cuz that's all you'll be getting," Mrs. Bosco mumbles under her breath.

We get to the Garden, and wait outside for everybody I've invited. Pretty soon, I start getting a bad case of the squigglies. People are shoving each other, and crowding around the entrance like it's Christmas or something.

"Tickets, tickets," whispers this scary-looking guy right in my ear. I look at him, startled, and he says, "You need tickets?"

"Um, no," I say, feeling scared.

"What's he want?" Chantelle asks me.

"He's a scalper," I explain.

"What's that?"

"That's people who sell tickets at a higher price," I explain to her, trying to calm down. Please, God, let our tickets be at the box office. Don't let this turn into Madison "Scare" Garden or something! If it's all a mistake, or if there's a mix-up and the tickets aren't there, I'll never live it down—I'll just sink into the ground and die of embarrassment!

"Look at all these people—they got free tick-ets, too?" Shawn asks me. I can tell he's kinda uncomfortable standing around.

"No, they didn't get free tickets—we did!" yells Twinkie loudly.

"Shhh, Twinkie," I say, holding her close.

"There's Monie!" yells Chantelle as my older sister approaches with her boyfriend, Hector.

"Heh, wazzup, Dorinda," he says, giving me a kiss on the cheek. "Thanks for inviting me." At least *he* has some manners. Maybe he should give Monie lessons.

I'm so happy when I see Galleria, Ms. Dorothea, Chanel, and Pucci walking through the crowd that I could jump up and down.

"Do' Re Mi, you are definitely pos-seeee!" riffs Galleria when she sees me. She puts out her hand so we can do the Cheetah Girls handshake.

Chanel is smiling as she walks through the crowd on her crutches.

"Coming through—can't you see she's on crutches?" Ms. Dorothea says sternly to the rowdy posse that's blocking their way.

Where is Tiffany, I wonder? She said her parents were gonna drop her off, but maybe they went to the wrong entrance or something. I mean, Madison Square Garden is supa-dupa big.

"You should've seen my mom's face this

morning when I told her," Chanel heckles when she's finally standing next to me. "She almost lost her balance belly dancing!"

"She practices so early in the morning?" I act surprised.

"*Sí, mamacita*—sometimes she gets up at six o'clock to exercise!" Chanel says, her eyes bugging wide.

"She's not coming?" I ask.

"No way, José! Her boyfriend is in town, and they're going to see *La Boheme*."

"Wow," I say, wondering what that is—probably something French, knowing Mrs. Simmons.

"Um, Mrs. Bosco, can you wait here with everybody while I go get the tickets?" I ask. See, I'm getting more and more scared and scared that the tickets won't really be there—and until I'm holding them in my hot little hand, I won't rest easy.

"Go ahead," Mrs. Bosco says.

"I'll go with you, Do'," Galleria volunteers.

When we see how long the line is at the box office, I get even more nervous. "We're gonna be here all day," I moan to Galleria.

"Hang tight," she says, running over to a

security guard. I can tell by the way she's giggling that she's angling for something. "This is the wrong line," she says when she returns, wearing a satisfied grin. "We've gotta go to the Will Call window."

"Word?" I say, impressed, because Will Call sounds kinda important.

"Will Call is where they keep all the Press and VIP tickets," Galleria informs me.

I'm still nervous as I walk up to the Will Call window and ask for the tickets. "Um, they should be under Dorinda Rogers," I say to the attendant.

"Excuse me," she says, not smiling, "you gotta talk louder."

"I said, *Dorinda Rogers*," I say, speaking up louder this time.

It seems like a thousand years are going by as we wait for her to flip through stacks of envelopes looking for our tickets. I can feel the sweat breaking out on my forehead and under my arms.

"Here you go," the attendant says, shoving an envelope through the window slot.

"Yippee-yi-yay!" Galleria shrieks, pinching my arm as I open the envelope and count the tickets.

"Don't let people see them!" Galleria adds, standing in front of me. "That guy over there is peeping the situation. This is the Big Apple—you know, they've got scalpers and pickpockets everywhere!"

"I know," I reply, embarrassed because I should know better. I shove the tickets into my backpack.

"Are we in business?" Galleria asks.

"Yeah!" Quickly, I count in my head all the people I invited, and the number of tickets I have in my backpack. Now I feel bad, because we still have some tickets left.

LaRonda and Tiffany are waiting with Chanel when Galleria and I get back. Tiffany is wearing the same white skort she had on the other day, but I don't say anything. I'm just glad to see her.

"Hi, Dorinda *mamacita*!" she says excitedly.

Chanel and Twinkie giggle at her Spanish.

"Wow, I like your hair," Tiffany exclaims to Twinkie.

"Thank you," my little sister says, beaming back. "You're Dorinda's sister?"

"Yeah," Tiffany says, looking at me for approval.

"You're the one with the keyboard?" Twinkie asks her.

"Yeah."

"Can I play it too?" Twinkie says, squinching up her nose.

"Oh, yeah—you wanna come over?"

"Can I?" Twinkie says, looking over at me.

"Don't look at me, Twinkie—she invited you," I say, chuckling. Now I can see that Twinkie and Tiffany are sort of alike, too—they both wanna get into the mix any way they can.

"Can I come over your house, for real?" Twinkie asks her.

"Yeah—you can come over for real!" Tiffany says excitedly.

Now I feel good that I'm not the only one who's got a new groove—it seems like my whole family, and the rest of the Cheetah Girls, are gonna get one, too.

"Girl, I can't believe we're going to see Mariah!" LaRonda pipes up outta nowhere. "You shoulda seen Derek's face when I told him."

"What did he say?" Galleria asks, chuckling. Even though she pretends she doesn't like the Red Snapper, we all know she does.

"His face was crushed, okay?" LaRonda

says, rolling her neck and pointing her index finger at the same time.

"I can't believe it, but I've still got tickets left," I say to Ms. Dorothea.

"That's fabulous—at least we'll have an empty seat to put our jackets on!" Ms. Dorothea says, satisfied.

"That's a real good idea, Ms. Dorothea!" Aqua says excitedly as we push our way through the entrance.

"Don't get *too* excited, darling, because my hat had better not get crushed!" Ms. Dorothea removes her big cheetah fake-fur hat.

"You should make those for your store," I yell to her.

"Are you kidding, Dorinda? I've gotta save a few head-turning designs for my private collection, or else I'd see myself going and coming all day!"

"You're right about that!" I chuckle back. Everybody copies Ms. Dorothea's designs, and some of her customers like to dress exactly like her—because Ms. Dorothea has the flavor that everybody savors, you know what I'm saying?

"Isn't this blazin' amazin', that *we're* at a

Mariah Carey concert?" Galleria riffs to Aqua as we make our way to our seats.

"Yes, indeed. We definitely have to give thanks to the Lord above," Aqua says, her big eyes popping.

"Well, I think the Lord would appreciate you giving thanks to Mrs. Bosco down here first!" Ms. Dorothea snipes.

We take our seats—which are about halfway back from the stage in the orchestra section. Soon, the place fills up, and we can all feel the electricity in the Garden as the lights go down, and the spotlights start roaming the walls.

"She's coming!" Twinkie yells in a shrilly voice, clapping excitedly.

The crowd starts chanting, "Mariah! Mariah! Mariah!"

"Do you think we should stick around to meet her afterward?" Galleria yells to me and Chanel as the crowd starts screaming with anticipation.

"It's worth a try!" Chanel says. "I mean, after all, Do' Re Mi and her family are VIPs—*está bien?*"

"You know who else are VIPs?" I say. "The Cheetah Girls!"

Galleria's eyes light up, and I can see how amped she gets by my attitude. "That's right, baby," she says. "Mariah's gonna help us fly—'cuz the Cheetah Girls are gonna *do* or *die!*"

Who's Got the Groove

We thought we had it goin' on
writing songs and gettin' along
that's Miss Chanel acting swell
and Galleria always freer
popping gum and acting glum
when the groove ain't right
and Toto bites with all his might!

Got a new member in our crew
Now she's got the rhymes
That's Miss Dorinda to you
Always true and
definitely crew
on the new school tip
without a slip

Who's got the groove?
Who's got the moves?
Miss Dorinda got it goin on'
till the break of dawn
she's riffing songs
or doing rhymes
on the banjo chords
and the mighty keyboard!

Who's got the groove?
Who's got the moves?
Miss Dorinda got it goin' on
till the break of dawn
So can't we all get along?
(I told you Tiffany is dope so let's cope and make
       her crew)
(Shut up, Chanel, before the copyright police
come and get you, mamacita!*)*

The Cheetah Girls Glossary

Angling for info: Being nosy.

Beef jerky: Static. A fight. A beef. As in, "Why she always trying to start a beef jerky with me? I'm not the one wearing a weava-lus hairdo, she is!"

Blazin' amazin': Phat. Dopa-licious.

Blow up your spot: When someone is trying to make you feel large or important. As in, "Did you see the way Loquanda was talking about you to Rerun? She was definitely trying to blow up your spot."

Bringing in the noise: Causing trouble. Acting rowdy. Or, having a good time and showing off your skills.

Brouhaha: A fight in a restaurant or a public place.

Buggin': Getting upset or acting cuckoo.

Diddly widdly: Nada. Nothing. Not even a crumb. As in, "I'm not giving her diddly widdly, 'cuz she wrecked my flow."

Dim-witty: Someone who needs to change the

lightbulb in their brain. Clueless, but definitely not a dum-dum.

Fib-eronis: Teeny-weeny fibs. Purple lies and alibis!

Get with the program: Figure something out. Go along with something. As in, "Loquanda and I are trying out for the track team—so you'd better get with the program, or you'll be hanging by yourself after school, okay?"

Good to go: Ready for Freddy. Ready for any thing!

Graveyard shift: That spooky time of night between midnight and eight o'clock in the morning, when most people are sleeping, except for "night owls," mummies, and vampires, or people who are working the graveyard shift. It is not to be confused with "Frankenstein Hour," however, which is when most mummies—alive or dead—come out of their grave for a little fresh air, 'cuz they've got time to spare!

Gunky: Dirty. Yukky. Like muddy water.

It ain't no thing but a chicken wing: It's cool. Everything's cool. Or, it could simply mean, *mamacita*, don't get too excited, it's just chicken!

Loco: Crazy. Cuckoo.

Lyrical flow: Someone who is good with words and writing songs, raps, or poems.

Milking for points: Taking advantage. Working it. As in, "Just 'cuz she got an A on the algebra quiz, she is definitely milking our math teacher for points."

My bad: Excuse me, I made a mistake. Oopsy, doopsy, this one's on me.

On the D.D.L.: On the down, down low. To do something without other people knowing about it. For example, "I want to make my mom a beaded necklace for her birthday, so I'm gonna have to do it on the D.D.L. so my brother won't give away the surprise." Can also mean, on the divette duckets license, which means buying something on the cheap.

Peeped: To catch on to something or pull someone's sleeve about something. As in, "I peeped Janessa cheating on the math test!"

Peep the situation: To try to figure out something. To look for clues to a situation.

Pickpocket: A sneaky bozo who goes around stealing wallets out of people's purses and pockets without them knowing it, then disappears faster than Houdini.

Plagiarism: Using someone else's words without giving them credit. In the case of songs, it can be very few words. For example, using the words *Living la vida loca* would qualify as plagiarism, since Ricky Martin already made that phrase famous in his song.

Radikkio: Ridiculous.

Right on the duckets: Right about something. As in, "You were right on the duckets. Crystal just told me that Tiara is not gonna show up. She left us hanging!"

Snarkle: A cross between a cackle and a giggle.

Stomping: Good. Dope. Tight. As in, "That song is stomping."

Street gravy: Gunky, dirty mud-filled water from the sewers.

What's the deal-io: What's the deal?

PHOTO BY CHARLIE PIZZARELLO

ABOUT THE AUTHOR

Deborah Gregory earned her growl power as a diva-about-town contributing writer for ESSENCE, VIBE, and MORE magazines. She has showed her spots on several talk shows, including OPRAH, RICKI LAKE, and MAURY POVICH. She lives in New York City with her pooch, Cappuccino, who is featured as the Cheetah Girls' mascot, Toto.

PHOTO BY TREVOR BROWN

 JUMP AT THE SUN

Hey, Girlfriend!

Would you like to be a member of our club?

Join Today!